Kite Music

Gary Shellhart

BANNED BOOKS

Austin, Texas

A BANNED BOOK

FIRST EDITION

Published in the United States of America
By Edward-William Publishing Company
Number 231, P.O. Box 33280, Austin, Texas 78764

ISBN 0-934411-07-7

Library of Congress Cataloging-in-Publication Data

Shellhart, Gary, 1947–
    Kite music.

    I. Title.
PS3569.H39362K5   1988   813'.54   88-960
ISBN 0-934411-07-7

1

There was a note at my desk when I returned from teaching my fourth year students. Ajan Prasit, the Headmaster of the college, wanted to see me at the temple later that afternoon. I looked forward to meeting him after his return from the Ministry of Education in Bangkok. As much as I looked forward to anything. There was a request for additional funds to teach evening classes I'd made, and I was eager for an answer. I wanted so badly to look like I was doing a capable job.

Besides, the visit with Ajan Prasit tended to leave me with a feeling of relaxation and renewal. *Ajan* means "teacher," the same title I shared while at the teachers' college. But with Prasit, the title took on more meaning than a man merely standing behind a desk; I was beginning to understand that the man taught by example, and did it with his every word and action.

I shuffled through some papers I'd have to correct that evening and stuffed them into a folder. I made a couple of notes. The way the ink blotted out over the paper reminded me of how sticky and hot I felt. It was the rainy season. I loosened my tie and ran a hand across my forehead, sweeping back my damp hair. I left the cluttered English Room to head for the stairs.

Students stood aside and bowed slightly as I passed. "Good afternoon, Ajan Peter," they said with shy smiles. I was just getting used to that, the respect accorded a teacher and an elder, although I was their senior by only a couple of years. I was on a teacher exchange program run by a group of West Coast colleges, and was based here in Northwest Thailand for two years. The junior college was far from Bangkok, in the provincial capital of Rio Et, training teens for a region hungry for new, young, and dedicated teachers.

For me, the opportunity beat getting drafted and serving in Vietnam. I was too absorbed in myself to have any strong opinions one way or the other about the escalating conflict in an area so close to where I lived, but it stirred mixed feelings in me — my country committing itself to what seemed mindless waste, while at the same time there was pride in knowing that America would defend vulnerable allies against Communist aggression. Seems I was wishy-washy on just about everything, damn it!

Walking the couple hundred yards to my stilt house got me hotter and sweatier. I glanced up to the water tower, the only landmark to rise above the village-campus. That tower had become a symbol to me for some reason, a stern structure standing solid and stark. In spite of meeting with Ajan Prasit to look forward to, I felt the tower staring down on me, judging my ineptness.

It stood there in the midst of the steamy jungle town, upright and unfeeling. I felt that same emotion I'd been nursing for my three months there emerging again. I felt vulnerable and useless. I had awaited my arrival in Thailand with ardent anticipation. But the reality of day to day life had hit me like a liquid fist, washing out my initial idealistic fantasies in a flood of alien sensations. After three months, I gritted my teeth and wondered if I should just admit my failure to make an impact here, submit a request to return home, and work on my post graduate degree in the familiar and predictable environment I'd grown up in.

A churning in my bowels reinforced the swirling despair in my head. A bout of dysentery had me feeling weak. I sensed that it was just an introduction of more insidious micro-organisms to come. I feared that my body was an inviting host to an army of parasites, just lurking about, waiting to drill into me and make me their home. There they would multiply and wreck havoc with my tissues and tubing, until, weak and fevered, I would be evacuated and treated in the air-conditioned comfort of a Bangkok hospital. I let the fantasy play out: friends would bring me milkshakes; they would feel sorry for me; I could order steak and maybe a cold beer; I could catch up on my reading.

My sad scenario was broken by a shout on my left. A soccer ball bounced up against the edge of the road and rolled to my feet.

"Here, Ajan Peter, send it here!" cried one of the boys on the field. It was a boy in my Second Year class. I didn't even remember his name.

I steadied the ball with the sole of my shoe, then gave it a kick with the side of my foot. My heart sank as I saw it wobble rather weakly over the soccer field. Not very good.

"Thank you, Ajan Peter!" grinned the boy, running to intercept the ball.

A sudden ache engulfed me as I watched him. In the midst of my resentment and self-pity, the youngster was so totally at home here, his vitality unchecked by self-doubts. He was beautiful, and his beauty hurt me deeply. His limbs were slim, his motions performed with unconscious grace. He ran sideways now, his feet busy at freeing the ball from the blurring feet of another boy, his arms flung wide for balance, his slender torso weaving — in complete control. His dark eyes were concentrated wholly upon the game, and his wide mouth set in concentration.

In spite of feeling so uncomfortable, I stood watching until a goal was scored. It was against my student's team, but the boy grinned just the same, extending his hand and embracing the long fingers of the boy who had made the point. The gesture was fluid, natural, and over in a second. I had seen so many like it before, a mere touch, done with casual accord. But this time a sadness welled up in me and

3

a knot tightened almost painfully in my throat. I felt loath-some, awkward, standing there watching such lithe beauty. I felt waxy-pale in my whiteness and stupidly huge compared to these Thai boys. I felt forever foreign and unwanted.

I clutched my folder in my wet hand and turned away, a swelling ball of misery pulsing up from my groin, spreading like chili-pepper heat. Tears burned at the bottom rims of my eyes. Pride and shame kept them from spelling over. I blinked rapidly, my feet plodding me up the stairs of my house.

I went to the kitchen and found that the ants had again invaded the cupboards. I locked down at the cups of water holding the legs; enough of the critters had drowned to form a bridge for others to follow. I swept a handful of the greedy little creatures aside and left the room in disgust.

The bedroom was messy. I opened the shutters and the stale air moved around. A slight breeze rippled through the mosquito netting surrounding my bed.

Then, unaccountably, there came the worst moment. Odd, how the most inconsequential thing can set off such a devastating reaction when the soul is primed for crisis.

It was the gnats. The tiny winged pests so small they were hardly visible until they buzzed around in front of my eyes. And it was there they flitted about, tingling against my eyelashes, mocking me with their mindless persistence. Their microscopic size merely justified my powerlessness. They seemed intent on burrowing into my eyes.

I stood stock still, tense in every muscle, aware of my world closing in on me, those pesky little gnats hovering about me as surely as vultures circle about a dying man. The heat became intolerable. I seemed to itch on every surface of my body.

I broke. A strangled sob ripped from my throat and I let it burst free from my tight chest. The emotion knocked me back, down onto the bed, where I sat with my head in my hands and let the bitter tears of self-pity flow freely. Goddam those gnats! Goddam the heat! Damn the endless flat plateau I lived on, without a hill or valley to break its

4

monotony! Damn those Thais for speaking their unintelligible language! Damn their fawning smiles and their stupid music, their endless patience and their silly dancing! And damn me for making such a foolish decision to come to this lonely place anyway!

The sound of water trickling to a flow came from the bathroom. The valve from the water tower was opened for only an hour or so each day, filling the troughs in each home for use through the next day. I had left the spigot open out of carelessness. That gave me another reason to continue whipping myself and I let the tears choke out in another gush of guilt.

Slowly, the tide of resentment ebbed. I felt somewhat lighter. I would take a shower, then would wait just a while longer before writing that letter of resignation.

By the sound of it, the water was at the top of the tank. I undressed and went into the bathroom. My vision and my thoughts cleared as I splashed bowl after bowl of water over me, being wasteful of it, then lathered from head to toe in sweet-smelling soap. I was unconsciously humming a Thai folk song as I rinsed off.

With clean clothes next to my skin, I walked to the temple to meet Ajan Prasit and found the low sun bathing the flat land in its ruddy light. It was almost beautiful. Clouds were building to thunderhead heights and a breeze blew from the southwest. I passed the ramshackle shops at the college gate and exchanged greetings with some students gathered there for snacks.

A bulldozer growled and screeched from the temple grounds. I saw it was plowing out a canal along one side of it, the temple building itself not yet half finished. The successful completion of the temple was Ajan Prasit's dream and passion, and the man was there whenever his duties as Headmaster allowed. And there he was, sitting crosslegged on a blanket on the bank of bare earth beside the building, serenely watching the clattering horsepower belching from the machine.

"Come, come, Ajan Peter. Sit beside me." He patted the blanket and I sat at his side.

We sat in silence for several minutes. The sound of the machine was too great to carry on a conversation, anyway. I looked over the temple, its brilliant red and green tiled roof and snake-like eaves already in place. The walls and pillars were bare plaster, however, awaiting further donations from the community for completion. I looked too at Ajan Prasit. He was rather small and frail, so calm. Yet I had come to know a power in the man. I often felt inadequate in his presence, yet he never did intimidate me. When, in my lonely evenings, I would visit him on the open veranda of his home, I would feel that things I questioned were made clear, although I had no active memory of Ajan Prasit teaching me anything I could accurately recall. He seemed to open pathways within me which would, given time, lead to the answers I sought.

"You had a good visit to Bangkok?" I asked when the bulldozer had moved away to the far side of the temple.

"Yes, yes. But it is so busy and noisy. An old country boy feels best when he returns to his home," he smiled.

I wondered if he knew how I felt, how badly just an hour before I had wanted to be home. I was too ashamed to tell him. "The workmen are busy," I said instead.

The Headmaster chuckled, his yellowing teeth showing. "That is why I am here, Peter. They work best when I supervise their progress! It is true for most people, like your students, yes? Do they not study more diligently when you are looking after them?"

I smiled and nodded.

"Will you have some tea?" Ajan Prasit asked, lifting a thermos and pouring some into a glass. He handed me the weak, steaming tea in his delicate fingers. I wanted to ask about the funds for evening classes, but I had become used to Ajan Prasit's method of conversation. He would not rush into the obvious. He would always try to draw a lesson from the immediate situation and put people around him at their

6

ease. Besides, I sensed that he had some other reason for asking me to come to the temple.

I sipped the musty tea, watching as he poured some for himself. He replaced the cork and turned to me.

"The machine is expensive. I am here also to ensure that the villager's investment is protected," he said without malice. "There are many in the Northeast who are poor, Peter. Many more mouths will pass before the temple is finished. There are many young people who wish to attend the Teachers' College, too. But they are too poor to pay the board when they leave their villages. It is sad, because they have such talent."

"Isn't there some government help, or scholarship money, for them?" I asked. I knew when I was assigned to the Northeast that it was the poorest of all of Thailand, and often its Lao-speaking people were scorned by their central-dialect countrymen.

"Such money was used the first term," said Ajan Prasit. "Twenty boys and girls were chosen from Roi-Et schools. But a friend tells me of some in villages on the river where the word of such funds never reached." Oddly, the man didn't look at all dejected about the information he was sharing with me. If anything, his kind eyes sparkled as he related the plight of these children who were denied their chance at education.

I thought about some of my neighbors, Thai teachers living in their stilt houses in clusters about the campus. "Don't some of the teachers have students living with them instead of the dormitories?" I asked.

"Yes, yes," he said softly. "But they must pay the student's board while he stays with them. And there are no more willing or able to do so."

"The college has provided me a good house, Headmaster. At home I was living in a small apartment before I came here."

The man sipped his tea. "I see you have few needs also, Ajan Peter. The money you receive from the Ministry, you spend it on food and books?"

7

"That and I'm saving some for trips," I answered.

"Will you travel alone?"

Alone. The word fit me. It had a hollow sound to it.

"I'm about the only teacher who lives alone, aren't I?" I asked.

Ajan Prasit nodded, his eyes following every move of the bulldozer as it reappeared around the temple, plowing up great slabs of muddy dirt.

A thought struck me. "I could take a couple students, Ajan. My house is large enough."

If I had time to consider the idea, it would have seemed ludicrous. I was so busy feeding my loneliness, any other people about would interfere. My restricting insecurity, my inability to share myself with others, would have stopped me.

Ajan Prasit grinned widely. "You have a very good idea there, Peter. And it is very generous of you to offer." The Headmaster paused for just a moment, then looked me in the eye. "Tonight will come two families with their boys. We will come to your home and discuss the arrangement at eight o'clock. You will see then if you can accept the boys." he held up his hand as though he were blessing the occasion.

I shook my head, grinning right back. The man was wise, yes, but he was ingenuously clever. He had arranged the whole thing beforehand. He'd induced me to come up with the idea he himself wished me to have. I understood immediately, too, how he must know of my loneliness. His unspoken compassion warmed me. If it worked, *my* idea would be a perfect solution for everyone.

"Oh, Ajan Peter, by the way, funds will be available for your evening classes next term."

Somehow the prospect of staying on another term seemed more tolerable after that meeting.

2

I was listening to Brahms on the cheap tape recorder I'd brought from Hong Kong when I heard voices approaching beneath my house. I sat, apprehensive and full of self-doubt. Shoes were removed at the bottom of my stairs and many bare feet approached my door.

"Come, come," said Ajan Prasit, waving the others forward with his open hand. He looked up to me and said, "They have arrived from the village, Ajan Peter."

They were a sad looking group. The mothers were clad in the mismatched colors of so many villagers, a blouse of one design and a *pasin* (the tubular garment around their waists) of another. Their bare feet displayed years of labor in the rice fields. They were cracked and the toes spaded out on the bottom. Their dark hair was pulled back into buns. It didn't occur to me at the time how terribly uncomfortable they must have been in the home of a foreigner, one passing judgment on their sons' futures.

The fathers were shy, sitting uneasily on my couch, while the two boys sat on the floor at the men's feet. One of the men seemed more at ease, but both were farmers, out of place, and eager to please. They didn't seem to know what to do with their hands.

I felt the same way. I shifted on my chair, hearing the thunder outside grow louder and more frequent. Thankfully, Ajan Prasit did most of the talking, and he spoke English with me. My Thai was very elementary still, and the villagers spoke the Laotian dialect which to my ears sounded like mush. The Headmaster introduced me to them all, adults first, then the boys.

"This is Wiboon," he said, holding his hand out to the larger one, "And this is Wichai." A flash of lightning lit up the room.

Both boys raised their hands, palms together, in a *wai*. I merely nodded, feeling nervous and insecure about all these people in my home, my refuge. It was, up till then, the one sanctuary away from everything, where I could be alone with my misery. Now, all that threatened to change.

My eyes stayed on the smaller boy for a moment, however. The corners of his mouth lifted in a shy grin and his eyes seemed to sparkle with mischief, as if her were peeking around his hands as he continued with the gesture of respect. The boy didn't look old enough to attend the college. To me he had the build of a twelve-year-old. His smile intimidated me, challenged me in a way I couldn't account for, and I couldn't smile back. He seemed to be someone I had seen at the edge of vision all my life, yet at the same time a stranger beyond knowing.

Ajan Prasit was talking to the families, and there was animated conversation for several minutes while my eyes went from one to the other. I avoided looking down to Wichai, but I felt he was staring at me the whole time. This habit the Thais had of staring sometimes made me want to shout at them, to yell at them for being so rude. How silly it all seems now, but at the time I wanted to make a face at the boy to shock him into looking away.

"So it is all settled," Ajan Prasit's voice cut through my fuzzy mind. "The boys will arrive for the next term beginning in a week. Their parents are very grateful for you, Ajan Peter. It is a great honor for their sons to stay with the American professor. That is satisfactory, Peter?"

I cleared my throat. "Yes, Ajan Prasit." What else could I say? This would be a first for me, never voluntarily living with others before. When I left home for college, I continued the loner ways I'd developed when first feeling that I was a

10

sexual pariah. I wasn't bitter or overtly hostile to a society convinced I was a deviate; I merely became quiet, resigned. Although the Headmaster was giving me the illusion of choice, sharing my home was something I felt was gently but irrepressibly forced on me, and was content to be submissive for the time being.

The mothers knew enough of what the Headmaster was saying for them to nod agreement and say something I didn't understand. I smiled.

Wichai's father was sitting close enough to extend his hand. I hesitated, not expecting a handshake. Feeling stupid, I grasped his calloused hand in mine. "Thank you," he said in a relieved voice, speaking the words in accented English.

As the troupe was leaving, Ajan Prasit turned at my door. Lightning flashed through the sky behind him. "You have made a very good decision, Ajan Peter," he said. "You will bring much happiness to the boys, and they will be good for you. You have been very wise." His grey eyes twinkled with something that looked like generous glee.

I plopped down on my chair and reached to turn up the Brahms, letting the thunder and the music wash away my tension. The image of Wichai drifted in and out of my thoughts, smiling boyishly, full of energy, tantalizing. That boy would fulfill the Headmaster's promise, more than I imagined.

3

Wiboon and Wichai arrived the following week, just as another downpour swept over the flat landscape. I saw them scurry under my house as I was pulling the shutters of my bedroom closed.

"Hello, Ajan Peter," the boys said, looking up. They just stood there as the rain pounded around them and we looked at each other dumbly. They each had a satchel on straps over their shoulders.

"Hello. Come up," I said. A gust of wind almost pushed them through the door, and we all struggled to close it. I felt confused, the monsoon storm clashing around the house, pounding on the tin roof. "I must close the windows," I said.

I rushed to the windows in the living room and leaned out to unlatch the shutters. I slammed them closed, my head dripping with rain. The boys rushed to the dining room to get the shutters there. Then we all went into the spare room where the boys would stay. We closed the room against the fury of the storm.

There came a loud crash from the dining room. We hurried there and saw that one shutter had blown loose and was slamming back and forth with the wind. Wichai reached it first, stretching out the window for the flapping shutter. It slammed back onto his hand. He jerked back with a yelp, bumping against Wiboon. Wiboon bumped against me and I staggered back, hitting the table. A pitcher teetered and fell to its side. I watched as it rolled to the edge of the table.

12

It fell. Just as it did, Wichai went to his knees and scooped it up in his hands.

We were all silent for a moment, looking at each other. Then Wichai smiled and held up the pitcher. "I save for you," he said.

I laughed! Wet and relieved, I thought the young boy's comment was richly funny. Wichai began to laugh also. Wiboon finally got the shutter closed and joined in, his eyes tearing as he looked at us almost doubling over. Soon we were all going in spasms of laughter as the storm raged about us.

"Welcome!" I managed to gasp, as I continued to laugh. "Welcome to your new home.!"

"Thank you, Ajan Peter," said the boys, giggling with delight. The tension was broken. I felt almost light-headed. It was a pure delight, this moment, after so many days of self-imposed despair.

"Show me your hand," I said to the smaller boy. "Did you hurt it?"

I sat in the chair beside him and Wichai held out his hand. I took it in mine. It was small and warm, wonderfully honey-tan. I felt a thrill at his touch. I didn't even then realize how hungry I was for the touch of another person, and this innocent contact was like a trembling jolt to my starved senses. I turned his hand over. His fingernails were small and neatly trimmed. The knuckles of his long fingers were barely wrinkled. There was just a slight ridge running over the back of his hand where the shutter had slammed into it.

I felt an unaccustomed sense of wonder surge through me as I held the boy's hand. I felt his large, dark eyes on me. I dropped his hand as if it were hot. "It is okay," I stammered. "I will show you to your room."

"Thank you, Ajan Peter," both boys said again, and we all stood.

The boys and I remained more or less strangers over the next couple weeks, all busy adjusting to the new term. I was pleased that both boys were placed in my first year class.

I came and went on my own schedule, sometimes finding Wichai or Wiboon or both at home, sometimes neither. When we returned from night classes, they usually went right to bed, tired from working in the experimental gardens as well as all their classes.

Each day, however, Wichai seemed to have a new phrase or question for me. I was hardly aware of it at first, but the delightful boy seemed to relish sharing with me a little gem his active mind had created.

"Ajan Peter, tell me about your home," he said one day.

Another day it was, "Ajan, look. A kite is flying over the fields. It is like a hawk soaring in the wind."

"Someday I will become a monk in my village," he said on still another occasion. "I will serve the temple for the honor of my family. I will learn how to live as a good Buddhist."

Wichai's voice had a husky resonance to it, a light purring quality which gave its high pitch a soft depth.

Little did I know then of the concentrated effort and time it took the boy to prepare such phrases in order to say them in perfect English. Well, almost perfect. He did it with such spirited innocence that I passed it off with casual interest. Yet the young boy intrigued me, brought out something protective and caring from deep within me. I found myself looking forward to these moments with Wichai. I found also that I was dwelling less and less on my self-pity and awkwardness. I stopped marking off dates on my calendar. Wichai was rescuing me from loneliness, and I hardly noticed.

Wiboon was more independent and self-assured. He was making his own friends, boys from other villages. While he spoke better English than Wichai, I found myself enjoying the company of the smaller boy and took him along on my frequent trips to the town market.

There was only one way to do it, since I had the only bicycle in the house. Wichai would sit side-saddle across the frame of the bike between my legs as he grasped the handlebars between my hands.

"I am too heavy, Ajan Peter?" he asked, turning up his head as I panted along.

"No, Wichai. You are very light."

Funny, how the sun's heat was less severe, the road shorter, and the trip to the market more pleasant with the boy there. I could smell him as he snuggled up against me on the bicycle, and his soft spicy scent was intoxicating. We laughed as we weaved about to avoid the large areas of soft laterite sand on the road into town.

"The horse is in the field," he said as we passed the race track. It was a line from the lesson the day before, and I got into the game with him.

"Man," I said.

"The man is in the field," Wichai parroted.

"Garden."

"The man is in the garden."

"Pig," I said as I eased the bike around a patch of dust.

"The pig is in the garden."

"Nose."

"The pig is in the nose," the boy said. He looked up sideways and frowned.

"The pig is in the nose," I said. "That's right."

Wichai muttered, then felt his nose. It was small and flat like all Thais. Then he looked up again. "The pig is in the nose?"

"Ear."

"The ear is in the nose. No, no, the pig is in the ear." Then he laughed. "Ajan Peter, where is the ear?"

I took one hand from the handlebars and pinched his ear. "Here it is, Wichai."

Then we started the game again. People learned to expect us to be together in the market, and began to ask me where Wichai was when I went in alone.

I became used to several changes as the boys stayed with me. Wichai would do the laundry, and we would all help clean the house. Wichai taught me how to care for the floors.

15

After a swarm of flying termites attacked us one night, Wichai was sweeping out the debris left by all their disconnected wings and writhing bodies. We swished the straw broom over the flooring where most fell between the planks, then continued out over the deck to fling the remains over the side. He wore his *pakama*, as he usually did at home, and hummed as I graded papers at my desk.

"Teak is very strong," he said as he reached to push his hair off his forehead. "It will shine and be clean if you put kerosene and wax on it."

I looked up, only half listening. "It's fine the way it is."

He smiled. "Ajan Peter, you are just lazy. You should be proud of your home."

"I'm proud of my job as teacher, Wichai. And right now I'm grading papers."

"You are a good teacher, Ajan Peter. But the floor is not good. It should be like in the temple."

"This is not a temple."

He thought a moment. "In English once, we read that a man's home is his castle. Is that right?"

I was both pleased and perplexed by the boy's tone. He lived here, too, after all, and I should realize his role in running the house. "Okay, Wichai. Let's shine the floor. But let me finish these papers first."

We were off to the market the next day on the school truck. It made a daily trip for meat and vegetables for the college cafeteria, and we loaded a tin of kerosene along with a block of candle wax for the return trip. The driver and the cook were glad to have us along, and showed us the best place to buy.

The day was fiery hot. Living in the tropics for several months had allowed me to adjust to the heat, but I felt it this day. But Wichai was eager to complete the project.

Wichai stirred the gas over a burner and added chunks of yellow wax to melt. The smell of it filled the house, strong and clean. When the blend was correct, he ran to the school to get some rags.

16

"We do this at home four times a year," Wichai said as we went to scrubbing the waxy gas into the floor.

"Your family must miss you while you are here at college," I grunted, slopping the planks and mopping it in. Sweat made my clothes cling to me.

"They know I must get an education, Ajan Peter. I am the oldest, and I must set an example for my brothers and sisters. I will graduate and get a teaching job, then help them to go to college, too."

"You want to be a teacher?"

He stopped in his work and whipped off his shirt. "Teachers help Thai students to be better citizens. And teachers have much respect, almost as much as a monk."

Wichai's civic pride almost wore a bit thin at times, and always made me feel rather selfish. But he was good for me, reminding me I was part of a larger community. I chose to turn the occasion into a joke, however. "Teachers have much respect, huh?"

"Oh, yes, Ajan Peter. And you have more than usual, because you are from America."

"Then why am I working like a servant, down on my knees waxing this floor?" I grinned.

Wichai responded in that adorable husky laugh of his. "Because we are proud of our house, Ajan Peter," he said.

And I was. We both ended wearing only our pakamas and thongs, admiring the gleaming surface of the teak floors, hard as marble and shiny as a temple's. We were gleaming with sweat ourselves.

"You take a shower first, Wichai," I said and sat to admire our work as I listened to the splashing of the boy pouring bowls of water over himself in the bath. The tiled room magnified the sound, which always was such a sibilant symphony to my ears. I imagined the boy's naked body, running with water, so close, behind the closed door. It seemed incongruent to me at that time that such a wiry little kid like that could hold such responsible plans for the future.

As I once again scanned the mirrored floor, I realized that waxing it was the first physical labor I had done in Thai-

17

land. I promised myself I would do more, especially if it could be shared with the boy.

One day Wichai was beaming with another question when I entered the house. He had just gotten out of the shower and was dressed only in his pakama wrapped about his slender waist with the knot tied casually in front. Water droplets beaded his tan skin.

"Ajan Peter, you know my favorite actor?" he asked, eyes dancing.

I guessed Paul Newman, Robert Redford, Jerry Lewis, and Mickey Mouse.

"No, no, no," said the boy. "My favorite actor is . . ." and he said something I couldn't understand. I sat and concentrated on his expressive lips as he struggled with what sounded like a slurring jumble. I had never seen his mouth so clearly before.

"Who?"

Again, it was just a confusion of syllables.

"Say it slower, Wichai."

Finally, I understood. It was Harold Lloyd! But with his Asian mixing of r's and l's the result was a fluid jumble, sounding to me like Hawowd Wroid! The boy couldn't have dreamed up a more difficult name. I burst out laughing! Poor Wichai looked hurt for a moment, then bubbled over into giggles with me, falling into my lap.

We laughed together in each other's arms. It was the first time I had held the boy. He was still damp from the shower, but his compact body felt wonderful as he cuddled against me over my lap. Our laughter softened and diminished as I held him. I ran my hand down his sleek back and lowered my cheek to rub against his wet black hair.

"You are like my father, Ajan Peter," said Wichai softly. He pulled his knees up and curled into a ball on my lap. I cupped his small body, feeling love for the boy in a way I'd never felt love for anyone before. I couldn't speak. The child was mystifying — he seemed so vulnerable yet energetic, so spirited yet so calm. I stroked his skinny shoulders and down his spine. Wichai shivered slightly under my touch and closed his eyes. Goose bumps formed briefly down his slim arms, then smoothed out again.

We stayed like that for many minutes. I lowered my lips and brushed them across his thick mane of hair. We breathed deeply, evenly. I felt more alive than I had in years, holding the beautiful boy, allowing him to trust me.

Wichai fell asleep in my arms. I almost cried. I felt silly about that, then dismissed the feeling as an old thought creeping back. I just let Wichai dream, his graceful body draped over mine. My eyelids felt heavy too. My fingertips feathered over Wichai's neck briefly. We slept together, holding each other, and did not wake up till Wiboon creaked the door open. He beamed when found us like that, so happy that Wichai and I were becoming friends.

4

Soon after that I again visited Ajan Prasit. It was evening, after dinner, and the Headmaster was pleased to see me after so many days. Fireflies were out in abundance, their twinkling green beacons spinning like a swarm of electrons around the bare electric bulb shining on his veranda. He served hot Ovaltine as we talked.

"Your night class, it is going well?" he asked.

"Oh, yes. Many students come after their chores. They are so eager to learn more conversation. All we have time for in class is drill." It was true, and I was enjoying the extra class in order to get to know some of the students better. Naturally, Wichai came with me and was the star of the class. Wiboon came also, and seemed to enjoy his friend's new enthusiasm. I never detected the slightest jealously in the larger boy.

"The Lord Buddha was very unhappy for a long time, you know," the Headmaster said. I sensed a lesson was beginning, and I was the willing pupil. I put down my cup and became more alert. "He was a prince with every luxury, but became bored and unsatisfied with life. He went on a pilgrimage and fasted. He endured pain and went without clothes.

"But he found that misery just made him miserable," Ajan Prasit said with a smile. "So the prince sought a way of life between the extremes. He meditated long and earnestly, hoping for an answer. He was enlightened and found the

20

Middle Path, Peter. He found that when he reduced his desires, they might be satisfied."

"Reduced?"

"He found that men are forever reaching beyond themselves, seeking illusions. Unsatisfied desires are the source of our suffering. The Buddha teaches us to find a true desire, perhaps the love for another, and devote ourselves to that, and to follow the Eight-Fold Path."

"I know some of those," I said. "What are they all?"

Ajan Prasit straightened somewhat in his chair, as though speaking at temple. "A man should live simply and practice right attitude, right thought, right speech, right behavior, right livelihood, right effort, right mindfulness, and right concentration, meaning meditation. A man who sincerely practices these things will not become angry or distracted by any harmful deed."

There was silence as we both lifted our cups and sipped the Ovaltine. I went back over what the man said about desires.

"I am confused, Ajan Prasit. Does Buddha teach that desires are bad?"

The man raised his eyebrows slightly and put out his hand. "No, no. There are many noble desires, Peter. I have noticed how close you and Wichai have become since he came to live with you." He paused, sipping from his cup. "The boy seems to love you."

I tensed. This was something secret, even to myself. I knew the prejudices against such a love. I had heard the snickers and derision from those in my own country against 'queers' and 'fairies.' But it was Ajan Prasit talking, not small-minded bullies from back home. I relaxed some and listened, nodding.

The Headmaster continued. "His is a pure and honest love. His desire to be loved is very real and precious."

I was struck dumb. Guilt swept over me like cold sweat. I dropped my jaw and began to protest. It was only respect of me as a teacher which gave that impression, I wanted to say. I knew my desire for the boy was . . .unnatural.

21

Ajan Prasit held his hand higher. "No, my friend, do not protest. It is an honest and human desire." He sipped his Ovaltine again, then added, quietly, "Do you love the boy?"

My spine twisted right up into my brain. I felt my tongue thicken, fear burn through my veins. Ajan Prasit patiently waited for the battle to rage within me. To declare my love for another male, that from childhood was so deeply instilled as insidious and corrupt. I had heard it condemned in church, school, and media as sinful, undesirable, an offense to nature and to man. Yet I felt it, as strongly as anything I had ever felt, perhaps more strongly for its having been suppressed. Say yes! my mind screamed. Admit it, open yourself to this man. Unscrew your emotions for a moment and risk the wrath of being different.

"Yes," I admitted.

A weight lifted from me. I leaned back in my chair, sucking in the warm, night air.

There was a moment's silence. A baby cried in a home not far away, and was soothed. My mind was beginning to slow its spin.

Ajan Prasit spoke again, with quiet force. "As long as you follow the Eight-Fold Path and do not abuse your love, it will bring you both happiness, and happiness to all those around you. I can already see that you are happier since the boy came to live with you. Your students are happier, too, Peter, are they not?"

I pictured my classes, rows of dark-eyed faces looking at me with more eagerness than in my first tentative weeks. He was right. I had been so busy thinking of myself and what others thought of me that I was unaware of how smoothly things had been going. So many things were new to me. I felt terribly naive.

"Feel proud that you have earned the love of another," said the Headmaster, "especially the love of a young boy. Such a love is very special and based on respect. It can be easily damaged, like holding a small bird in your hand. Do

22

you remember how hurt you were as a boy when someone you looked up to disappointed you?"

My memory rolled back to a point when I was a sophomore, about the age Wichai was now. "There was an older boy," I said. "I felt he was perfect. I even tried to walk like him," I laughed nervously. "Then he made fun of me in front of some other people." The sting of it still hurt, after years.

"You must be aware of the boy's feelings, too, for he looks up to you. Love is a great risk for him; it is a new experience for one so young. The boy has never been hurt by someone he loves, so he trusts you completely."

The man's words were like a soothing breeze through the warm evening. The fireflies were fewer now, their cool green lights blinking erratically. I finished up the thickened Ovaltine and felt more sure of myself than for a long time. The boy's own words occurred to me.

"You are like a father to me," I said to the Headmaster, as Wichai had to me. "No one has ever told me of the responsibilities of love before. It *is* a great responsibility."

"It is a great adventure, Peter," smiled Ajan Prasit. "Do not worry. The Buddha says, 'Do not dwell in the past, do not dream of the future, concentrate the mind on the present moment.' "

When I returned to my own home, I found Wichai sitting slumped on the couch, his elbow up on the arm of it with his hand holding his nodding head. A science book lay open on his lap. He was dressed only in his faded pakama.

I sat and watched the boy for a long time, thinking of what Ajan Prasit had said, ordering my own feelings as best I could. Wichai was the most beautiful, most desirable thing I'd ever known. His mind was as agile as his body was supple. His humor was spontaneous and bright. Yes, I loved him.

I ran my left hand beneath his firm thighs. I ran my right behind his back. I pulled the boy into my arms and stood.

"Mmmmmmm, Ajan Peter," mumbled the sleepy boy, his eyelids fluttering half open. "I sleep."

23

I looked down on Wichai, so innocent and trusting. "Yes, I think you should go to bed."

I cradled Wichai in my arms and walked to his room. Wiboon lay asleep with his back to us in the far bed, with just moonlight glowing in the small room. I felt Wichai's arms encircle me. He rubbed his cheek against my chest like a cat. I looked down and saw the knot of his pakama had worked loose. The boy didn't move to cover himself as the cloth fell from his waist and dangled free. The youngster was naked down one side, the thin cotton just covering his groin in careless folds.

We embraced. One or both of us trembled. I was living totally in the moment, a beautiful young boy breathing against me. I formed the words, "I love you," with my lips against his hair, but couldn't say them aloud, not in English or Thai. Not yet. I moved to the bed and Wichai held out his hand to part the netting.

Supine over the single bed, the boy still didn't cover himself. He looked up at me, his face without expression but his dark eyes filling up the world. "Wichai loves Ajan Peter," he said in a firm, quiet voice.

The boy seemed without sophistication, without all the futile doubts I let hamper my own emotions. I felt a throb of envy mixed with wonder at his simple words. And I couldn't respond! I stood there, mute and foolish, dazed by Wichai's simple declaration of his feelings. He asked nothing, demanded nothing. He simply loved me!

I reached out and drew the gossamer netting closed. The boy and I looked at each other briefly through the gauze-like barrier.

"Good night, Wichai," I whispered, and turned to go to my own room. It was a long time before I could sleep.

5

"Look, Ajan Peter!" cried Wichai as I pulled my bicycle onto the concrete slab under our house. "Look, I finished weaving my takraw ball!"

He jerked up his knee and sent the ball springing up high off it. As it arced down, he lifted his foot sideways and met the ball with his heel. It flew up again. He did it over and over, hopping in place on his left foot, bouncing the rattan ball high up off his ankle. He grinned proudly as I leaned my bike against the stairs and applauded his nimble talent.

Wichai had such a careless way of throwing himself into physical activity. He seemed to be in such graceful control, and totally unafraid of hurting himself with his youthful energy. I stood and watched, astonished by his boyish joy. His bare legs were long and thin, pirouetting with unconscious ease to fling the ball he'd made into the air again and again.

"Here, you try!" he said, and sent the ball flying toward me. I lifted up my leg as he had, met the ball, and whacked it sideways. It slammed up into the rafters of the house, bounced down on the ground, and rolled off the slab. It came to rest between the front legs of our neighbor's water buffalo.

"Get it, Wichai!" I yelled as the animal lowered its head to sniff the unfamiliar object. The huge animal opened its jaws just as the boy swooped down and snatched it away. He gave the animal a friendly pat on its fat side and walked

25

back admiring the ball he had weaved together himself. He shook off the dust and looked up at me, his head cocked a bit.

"You are not so good, Ajan Peter," he said with a mischievous grin.

I laughed. A couple months earlier I would have reacted so differently, but the youngster was so charming in his honesty that I had to laugh. And he was so right, too. I had marveled at the skill, the artless grace, of boys as I watched them play takraw, using feet, elbows, shoulders, and heads to send the ball over a net something like volleyball, their tan skins gleaming with sweat, their lean muscles sprung tight.

Well, such sport requires admiring spectators, too, I thought.

We went upstairs and opened a couple Cokes, relaxing after the day at school. Wichai went to the map of the world I had hanging on the living room wall. I watched as his long brown fingers touched the western United States.

"Ajan Peter, what is the weather where you live?"

It struck me that I hadn't thought of home for a while. "Well, it's November. The weather is getting cold, the trees lose their leaves, and the sun shines only about seven or eight hours a day. Sometimes it snows this early, too."

Wichai crinkled up his nose. He did that when he thought hard. "Snow, Ajan Peter, what is it like?"

"It's very cold and white and fun to play in." I leaned close to the boy, spotting the mountains where I used to go skiing. I could feel the heat of his body, smell his musky sweat. "Everything is beautiful and the schools close because it is like a flood and people can't travel. Children are free to play in the snow."

"Someday I will visit your home, Ajan Peter."

I rested my hand on his back, then gently rubbed over his shoulders. His thin t-shirt was damp. "I hope so, Wichai. I like living in your country."

The boy's eyes scanned the long journey west across the Pacific to Thailand on the map. Then he turned to look up at me. "You have not visited my family home yet." Wichai paused and ran his tongue slowly over his lips. "You will come for the festival of Loy Kratong."

It was not a question. And before I could respond, he continued: "It is a beautiful festival, Ajan Peter. My family wants to see you again and welcome you to our home. We will take a bus to the river and go by boat. The road is very bad."

"What about Wiboon?" I asked.

"It is his village, too. He will come with us to visit his family."

I cupped the boy's shoulder with my fingers, then lightly touched the fine hairs at the nape of his neck. Again, tiny goosebumps rose over his smooth skin, and the boy seemed to quiver under my caress. My love for him was growing, there was no stopping it. It ached in me now, and the ache was painfully sweet.

"Okay," I said, giving him a gentle squeeze. I rose to take a shower.

I reported to Ajan Prasit that I was going to visit Ban Tawatburi with Wichai. The man was pleased, wishing me a pleasant trip. He was on his way to the temple, so we didn't talk long. But the man's serene assurance filled a vacuum in me I hardly knew was there before.

The rains began to ebb, clouds parting at night to reveal a moon swelling to fullness, the time of Loy Kratong. Wichai was eager as a puppy once we got underway. I rode the bike with him sitting over the frame while Wiboon followed on one he'd borrowed, our bags dangling from the handlebars.

"My father is a rice farmer, like most Thai people," chattered Wichai. "But he is also a village doctor," he said proudly. "He goes from village to village to help the sick people. My mother, she spins silk. She grows the silk worms herself! She will show you, Ajan Peter."

"And your brothers or sisters?" I asked, panting as I peddled along the dirt road. I realized how little I knew about the boy I was falling in love with. I was ashamed, then suddenly strongly curious. I wanted to know everything about Wichai and his world.

27

The boy had two sisters and three brothers, all of them younger. "Maliwan is the youngest. She has not had her hair cut yet. It is a ceremony for the first year of life. You will like my family. I will be proud to help them when I can send them money for their education."

It struck me odd how this sense of responsibility existed side by side with Wichai's playful enthusiasm. Then I remembered how he spoke already of serving in the temple, to learn to live as a monk and to bring honor to his family. I had much to learn.

After the clattering bus ride, we had to wait some time at the River Chee, at the bridge where we would take the boat downstream to Ban Tawatburi. An American jet fighter screamed overhead, followed by two others, returning from Vietnam and winging just over the treetops. They seemed to get a daredevil thrill by going so low after the dangers they had faced over enemy territory.

After the bumps and sways of the bus ride and as the thunderous jets droned into the distance, the river scene seemed blissfully silent, as though insulated from all the machinery of man. The boys and I sipped orange sodas as the river life unfolded below. Our boat was lazily loaded with bales of dried jute. Its swampy smell used to repel me; now it filled the air like pungent perfume.

Several villagers squatted on the bank with us, awaiting boats up or down river. The men were dressed in dark blue cotton, with checkered pakamas tied around their waists and thongs on their weathered feet. The acrid smoke of their home-grown cheroots blended with the smell of jute. The women had pasins, long colorful tubes of cotton, knotted at their waists, and mismatched blouses. One was nursing an infant, leaning to the side to spit as she chewed and spat her betal. Two of her other children clung to her, hands on her shoulders, staring at me.

"Why do Thai people stare so much?" I asked. This habit had irritated me, especially when I first arrived. Now it merely amused me, and I felt that Wichai wouldn't be offended by my curiosity.

"You are different, Ajan Peter." He motioned the little girl and boy over to us and reached into his pocket.

"I know I'm different," I answered. "But it is rude to stare like that."

"They are not rude. They are curious." He took out a button with string run through its holes, holding it up in front of him. Without changing his expression, he tugged the ends of the strings and started the button whirling.

"See, they are now curious about my toy," he said. The button was now a blur, and the whirring sound fascinated the children. They imitated it by blowing air through their lips as their wide eyes stared at Wichai's toy dancing between his hands.

Simple, I thought. "Yes, I see."

The whistle blew and we climbed aboard. Wichai sat firm against me on the small bench at the front as we got underway, the long-shafted engine sending up a rooster-tail in our wake.

"The best view is in front, Ajan Peter," the boy said. He didn't mention that the spray of water was the greatest there, also. We threw back our heads and showered in the warm mist spraying up over the bow, laughing, as the boat sputtered over the swollen waters.

We stopped from time to time along the muddy river bank, loading and unloading people and cargo. The jungle growth was the richest I'd seen in my stay in Thailand.

"See the buffalo boys!" Wichai shouted, pointing. The boat slowed as we rounded a wide bend, passing a small herd of water buffalo wallowing in the shallows, their broad backs shining black just breaking the surface. Their dramatically curved horns turned with their heads as they watched us pass, their huge eyes slowly blinking. In the water up to his knees was a young boy, totally naked, waving at us. His honey-tanned skin gleamed in the tropical sun, his lips wide in an open smile. His tiny penis hung cutely between his slender legs, dripping water.

Another boy, equally naked, sat astride one of the big animals, his thin legs dangling out over the girth of the water

29

buffalo's wide back. His tiny buttocks rested lightly over the tough-skinned animal, and he waved also.

"I took care of the buffalo when I was young," said Wichai. "It is fun to get into the water with them after working in the rice fields."

I turned to watch the buffalo boys as we rounded the bend of the river. I wanted a final glimpse of their unadorned beauty. I say them turn their attention from the passing boat to splashing each other, cupping their hands in the silty water and raining it over each other's slick bodies. The motor drowned out the high-pitched giggles I could see rippling through them.

I wiped some spray off my face and looked again at Wichai. He had one small hand on my thigh, I rested one also on his, almost to his groin. I pictured him as a nude young water buffalo boy, legs splayed over the animal and dripping wet. I pictured him fully erect, his penis lifted up against his belly, a look of quiet need burning in his dark young eyes, his lovely lips parted with abandoned lust.

God, how I'd fantasized over such a picture. I read the diaries of Andre Gide with a passion, wondering if I could ever know such ecstacy as he did in North Africa. My copy of *Death in Venice* was likewise dog-eared. I'd once come across a book by a man named Michael Davidson, an odyssey of boy-love around the world. I'd burned it in a fit of guilt.

The wave of passion surged through me. I wondered if my love for him could be contained, or if I would overstep the bounds of responsible love if my desire for him became too great. Confronting my lust for the first time, with Wichai as the subject of it, I was shocked by its intensity. I drew my hand off him and held on to the side of the boat, looking away. Wichai kept his warm hand where it was.

Wichai's village wasn't obvious from the river. A well-worn path down the muddy river bank was all that marked the spot where Ban Tawatburi lay in the jungle beyond. Wiboon, Wichai, and I scampered up the oozy trail and I followed the boys toward their home. Soon, simple stilt houses appeared along the path, which opened into a central clearing, with the homes more or less parallel to the river. Coconut and betel palms, banana plants, clumps of bamboo, and ornamental shrubs surrounded each house. A few dogs roamed about, barking at our arrival. Wichai called one by name and its tail went wagging.

Wiboon went his way to his family while Wichai and I approached his home. We walked into the compound through a simple bamboo gate and we merged with the daily life of his family.

Any apprehension I harbored over meeting the boy's family after our first nervous encounter was soon dispelled. His mother smiled as we bowed to each other and *waied*. She sat on a low stool spinning silk under the house. Small yellowish balls of raw silk lay on wide straw discs where they had dried after boiling. She was working a simple spinning wheel, her rough bare foot pumping it with a steady rhythm, drawing the strong threads out of the fuzzy masses.

"Welcome, Ajan Peter," the woman said simply. "You must stay her often with Wichai. He writes to us that you are a very good man."

I felt heat rise up my neck and over my cheeks. "Thank you, Mrs. Maliwan," I stammered. My Thai was becoming more fluent, but her words were difficult for me, I was as yet so unsure of myself.

Wichai spoke in his rapid Laotian dialect with her for a few minutes in his wonderfully resonant young voice. I caught an occasional word, then he turned to me and said, "I told her how you are a very good teacher and friend. How you are kind, and how I love you. She is very happy her son has such a good *farang* friend," he said, using the Thai word for foreigner.

"My son is good in his studies?" she asked, in Thai.

"Yes," I said. "He is very diligent."

There was a silence which I felt was awkward. It made me aware of how silent the village was, though, with only the rustle of wind through the palm fronds overhead.

"We are dusty and dirty from traveling. Let's shower, Ajan Peter," piped in Wichai, his light fingers touching my

31

arm. the boy took my hand and led me up the steps of their house to empty our bags and get out our pakamas.

"Someday you must see what it is like to be a rice farmer," Wichai said as he tied the knot of his pakama.

"I'm afraid I wouldn't be very good. When I planted vegetables at home, I always forgot to weed and water them."

"Then I will teach you," he said.

In the small enclosure of bamboo behind the house was a well with a concrete pad surrounding it. Wichai and I poured bowls of cool water over ourselves, then lathered up with soap, our pakamas drawn back up between our legs and tucked in at the back, looking something like pantaloons. I threw back my head and splashed the clear water over my head, feeling its trickling path down my chest and back, then running down my legs. Neither of us talked much, just sighed with the pleasure of cool water cutting through our grimy heat.

"Soap my back, Ajan Peter, please," said the boy, his thick black hair falling damp down his forehead. He turned and I ran my hands over his back. I rubbed suds around his delicate shoulder blades and down his spine. My hand trembled as I touched his smooth skin. The boy's pakama came loose where it was tucked in at his back. Still encircling his slender waist, the wet hem of the garment fell down about his legs as I washed over the small of his back. He just stood, eyes lowered, letting the cloth flap, dripping, to his knees.

I tore my eyes away from him and looked up. "Look, Wichai, the moon is already rising."

"And look," he said as he raised his arm to point. "You can see the rabbit in the moon."

I slid my hand up his side, into his armpit, then over the length of his arm to his fingers. "Rabbit?" I asked. "I see a man in the moon, but not a rabbit."

"Turn your head," he said, doing it himself.

I imitated him and there it was, the obvious profile of a rabbit, ears and all.

"Do you want to hear a story of the rabbit in the moon, Ajan Peter?"

"Tell me." I kept stroking his arms and shoulders, then around his neck.

"The Lord Buddha was on a pilgrimage, disguised as a poor old man. One night he came to a place in the forest and built a small fire to keep warm. A rabbit saw the old man. He wanted to feed him because he looked hungry."—I was massaging the boy's back now as much as washing it—"but he had only vegetables. The old man looked like he needed meat. So the rabbit threw himself into the fire."

I rested my hands on Wichai's bony shoulders and looked up again at the moon.

Wichai continued. "The Lord Buddha put its image on the moon to remind us to sacrifice for each other to make merit."

I thought about it, what I could do for the boy. Instead, he turned and said, "Now I will wash you, Ajan Peter."

I turned and felt Wichai's firm hands massage slick soap over my back. A tingling thrill ran down my spine. An insect buzzing seemed to fill the air. The boy hummed as if purring as he rubbed over my pale skin, reaching up to work his fingers into my shoulders. Tension flowed out of me, and a warmth enveloped the air about us.

He stooped and I turned. Wichai's pakama had slipped from his thin hips and lay in a soggy bundle at his feet. The boy was totally, wonderfully bare. We stood there, dripping and sudsy, close to each other, Wichai gently looking up into my eyes.

He was lovely beyond words, and more desirable than any fantasy I could imagine. He stood casually, vulnerable, and exposed, his slender nudity open to my gaze, to my touch. I felt paralyzed. It was as if the terrible power of love was leashed tight by a force of equal restraint.

I reach out to touch his cheek. He turned his head into my caress, rubbing his face into my open hand. Tiny, shiny-colored bubbles slicked over his tan skin. Wichai hummed deep in his throat as I cupped his face in my palm. It was an unaware dream come true, the boy naked and aroused, aching for my touch. I felt tremors vibrate through us, and it reminded me of Ajan Prasit's words, "like holding a small bird in your hand." I felt defenseless against the awesome powers tugging at my heart, sensed that Wichai was equally defenseless under my caress.

I traced around the rim of his ear, pushing back his hair, then lightly held the rubbery little lobe of it between my thumb and finger. I moved my hand over his forehead as though examining fine sculpture, his wet hair brushing over my knuckles. I ran my fingers down between his wide eyes over the bridge of his nose. I felt his soft lips with my fingertips, stroking over them back and forth. He let his lips open, relaxed. His eyelids fluttered, then closed.

I looked down over the boy. Wichai was so thin, his ribs showed through his firm chest. His stomach was flat, sinking in with his even breathing. He was hairless except for a slight furring around his small erection. I brushed over his lips and his cheek again and the youngster quivered, his tiny toes curling under. I realized that he may be on the brink of orgasm!

"You are beautiful!" I gasped. I was half-hard, throbbing in the confines of my pakama. A burning ball of emotion churned in the pit of my stomach.

I pinched Wichai's button nose and he sputtered, then giggled as I drew my fingers down over his chest and sides, tickling him. I sucked in my breath deeply — feeling something in me stretched so tight, it almost snapped. It frightened me. My senses seemed overloaded, bursting.

I bent down to grab the bowl, then swung up with it, spraying the boy with water.

Wichai retaliated, cupping up water in the palms of his hands and showering me in streams of it. It was like we were buffalo boys, I thought. The whole village must have heard our shouts and laughter. His penis softened some with our play, and soon he was wrapped in his pakama again and we were walking back up the stairs to his house to dress.

As evening approached, the village seemed to flow harmoniously into activity. It was like pulling the string of a loose puppet, and all the pieces drew together and worked as one. Charcoal fires were lit and fanned till they blazed. Food was prepared. And the small floats for the festival were assembled.

I sat, mesmerized, on the veranda, watching Wichai's mother pluck feathers from the chicken his father had killed for dinner. The sun's rays were low and golden-red. Wichai sat beside me, working banana leaves into small lotus-shaped boats, securing them with sticks of wood he sliced from a block of teak with a cleaver.

Wichai worked with relaxed dexterity, making a kratong float for each member of the family, and one for me. As the sun set, a single oil lamp was lit and the wok was soon sizzling with chicken and vegetables, sending out a rich and spicy scent over the still night air around us.

"We celebrate Loy Kratong when the water is high," said Wichai in answer to my questions as we ate. "First we visit the temple, then go to the river to float kratongs out onto the water. Into them we put a candle, a coin, and incense."

"What does it mean, Wichai?"

"It is to honor the spirit of the water." He paused, his brow temporarily rippling in thought. "Some believe that it is to wash away our sins. But we have no sins yet, Ajan Peter." I swear the boy winked.

We ate, Wichai's younger brothers and sister wide-eyed and silent, his mother or father sometimes talking briefly with me and each other between mouthfuls of sticky rice and pungent chicken. I found that I was more at ease than ever, hardly noticing as the conversation now went from English to Thai, even into some Laotian. We were just friends sitting around on the veranda sharing a delicious meal. Wichai's smiles of approval washed away all apprehensions.

6

After the meal we took the kratongs Wichai made to the temple. As we left the simple ceremony there, we merged with other families shrouded in darkness. I stayed close to Wichai. There was a comforting mumble of Laotian as we moved on the path to the river.

"Hi there! The kid's family said there was another farang in town," came a voice behind me on the darkened path. I jumped. The voice was distinctly American. I turned.

In the light of a candle I spotted a sandy-haired man in his late twenties, I guessed, wiry and grinning through his whiskers at my surprise.

"Who are you?" was all I could think of to say. I got a whiff of Mekong whiskey off him.

"Just a friendly yank among the heathen," he snorted. Then he put out his hand. "Ben Ferrall's the name. Kind of startled you, didn't I?"

"Peter Carpender," I said. His grip was almost desperately firm.

"Mr. Ben stays with my family for many weeks now," said Wiboon, walking at the man's side. "He is a brave American soldier."

My first thought was he might be an anthropologist or such. But soldier fit him. He had the straight spine and swagger of a GI. "A soldier? Here?" I was immediately on guard. The last thing I expected to find in the village was another American, and a soldier at that.

Ben waved his hand in front of his face several times, nodding his head. "Let's get on to the river, buddy. I'll explain later."

I felt Wichai slip his hand into mine. I leaned down as he put his mouth to my ear. "I think Mr. Ben is tired of being a soldier. Wiboon's family found him wandering in the rice fields and brought him to the village. He was very tired, kind of crazy."

We emerged from the jungle and faced the river. The full moon's light bathed the scene in a ghostly white. Already there were flickering candles lit and placed in the little lotus boats. Ben returned to my side. "Sorry if I took you by surprise back there, buddy. I told the boys to keep me secret, and I guess they did their job."

I shrugged my shoulders. "Well, they kept your secret. What are you doing here, anyway?" Frankly, I was jealous as well as startled. I figured Wichai brought me to his village as the exclusive outsider to the place, and sharing the turf with this forceful stranger had my stomach churning.

Ben ignored my question. "Pete, you been living in Thailand long?"

"Only about five months. This is my first visit to a village."

The man sighed, then grunted. "Peaceful place. Been through hell in Nam. Don't know if I can go back, buddy. Don't know. . . ." He seemed confused. His eyes strayed to the water and were berry-bright with the pin-points of reflections off the candles.

I touched his arm and he jumped. I drew back, seeking to see what was happening in those intense eyes of his. They were wide now, and frightened. I realized instinctively that Ben was like two people — one sane and friendly, the other scared and suspicious. Just as I was about to turn back to Wichai, he spoke again.

"Been in Nam for over two years, Pete. Been fighting from Saigon to the DMZ. Through villages like this one here. Leaving 'em nothing but husks — dead, dead, dead."

37

I felt itchy. Voices of concern came from the villagers watching us.

"Started out brave and simple, knowing the enemy as a dog knows a scent. But it's not like that, not like my daddy told me. He fought in the big one, WW Two," he snorted, "and he told me how right was right and wrong was wrong. Hell, it ain't like that. Right and wrong don't matter. . . ."

"We're fighting against the Communists, aren't we?" I asked. I was reminded that my motives for working in Thailand were less than noble. I'd had doubts about the war, sure, but I wanted to get something that would defer me from the draft until the whole thing blew over.

Ben bared his teeth and spat. He wrung his fingers till his knuckles were wrinkled and white in the pale light. He didn't answer with more than those gestures. I felt the man was a threatening force, his bitterness so overwhelming, so self-justified. I could smell the scent of death on him. And I feared getting involved with a man I knew was probably AWOL at best, a fugitive at worst, holed up here a full country away from his command. He was a threat to my idyllic isolation.

Ben grabbed at my arm again, clutching it. He spoke low and urgently. "Peter, buddy, you must keep my presence here super hush-hush. Don't tell anyone you saw me, not even saw a fucking yank. You got that? I got to stay here till I get things sorted out."

"You deserted, didn't you?"

Ben sucked in his breath. "Let's just say that after fighting shadow-gooks in Nam and seeing no fucking good in it for a couple of years, I got tired, fucking tired of the whole fucking thing. Pete, I just couldn't take the killing, and the lying, and the crazy gung-ho shit anymore. And the war's changing, too. The new kids coming over, they got no idea what they're doing. They think—oh, hell, what's the use?"

The man's voice broke. "And I'm into things I can't get out of any other way, Pete. I can't just plead my case, cop a medical or something, and get a transfer out."

"What do you mean?" I was getting impatient. The people gathered at the water's edge began to look at us as if the ceremony couldn't begin until there was some peace between us.

"Can't tell," he snapped.

I tried to shake his fingers off my arm. He gripped tighter.

"I killed a child, Pete!" he hissed. "A fucking *child!*"

"I'll zip my lip, Ben. But what are you going to do? You can't stay in Tawatburi forever."

Just then Wichai's sweet voice came from the river bank. "Ajan Peter, come. Your kratong."

I shook off Ben's hand, now limp, and went to the boy. I took the floats he held out to me while he struck a match and lit each candle within them, then each stick of spicy incense. His face was lit by the flame's warm glow, the reflections glittering in his large, dark eyes, so full of peace. Then Wichai took one and we sent them with a push over the smooth surface of the slow-moving water.

Soon scores of dancing flames bobbed over the swollen river, their reflections snaking down in long, fluid ripples. Wichai and I sat on a straw mat, touching, watching the moon-washed parade of lights. A Northeastern instrument called a *kan*, a pan-pipe fashioned of bamboo, played some distance away.

I should have been alive in the moment, as I had been before. The world, Ben, and the war should have been erased by the idyllic simplicity of the scene before me, and Wichai at my side.

Instead, I was irritated. Ben had spoiled something which was entirely my own. The mosquitoes buzz-bombed me in the night and I felt itchy all over. To top it off, I grew upset with Wichai.

"That man, he is dangerous, isn't he, Ajan Peter?" he asked.

"I don't know. He seems confused, that's all."

"Do you want to be a soldier?"

"No," I said, whipping at the mosquitoes. "Do you?"

"I want to be a teacher, like you. I want to everything like you, Ajan Peter."

I stood in frustration and walked away from the boy, toward the river, then turned. "I am not perfect, Wichai. I do many things wrong. You have to be yourself, not someone who just comes into you life and leaves again."

"But you are a good man."

Damn, the boy had me confused. How could I confront the boy with reality without destroying his faith in me? I didn't want him to admire me as he would a magazine photo.

I looked from the flame-dotted river back to him on the bank. His delicate form was outlined in the silver of the moon. It hurt me to want to hurt him, but the mood overwhelmed me. Before allowing him to reply, I continued. "You should not just copy some just because they are American. That's what's wrong with you Thai, you want to be just like Americans so you imitate them, the way they dress, their music, all that stuff."

"You are mad at Thai people?"

"Sometimes. Maybe I'm just homesick, Wichai. But there are things I'll never like here. Like these bugs," I said, swatting at a stinger on my arm.

There was hurt in Wichai's voice as he answered. "But I think you are a very fine person. I want to teach and travel like you. What is wrong in that?"

"Nothing," I sighed. "Let's get back to the village. I'm tired."

"My family thinks you are a very fine person, too," he said as I followed him along the path.

"They are good people," I said. And I meant it. In fact, they seemed too good, and my own weaknesses, my lust after their son, made me all the angrier.

As we cleared the brush, the village emerged like a black and white negative in the border of darker palms. A hand caught my arm as we neared Wichai's house.

"Sssst, Pete. It's Ben again. Can we have a chat?"

"Don't grab me like that!" I spat as I shook off his hand.

"Yes, we can have a chat." Then, gentler, to Wichai, "You go on ahead. I'll be there in a few minutes."

Ben headed a little unsteadily over to the base of a palm and leaned against it. I followed him, and saw his haggard face glow in the light of a match. The acrid fumes of marijuana drifted over the still air.

I was still miffed. "What do you want, Ben? I don't have anything to do with your affairs, and I won't tell anyone I saw you."

"They're already after me," he said simply.

"The army?"

"CID." He saw I didn't understand. "That's Criminal Investigations Division. Heavy stuff."

"Why don't you just go back now and explain that you went, well, crazy for a while. That you didn't do anything stupid. I'm sure you aren't the first one in this war to do that."

Ben snorted, then drew the smoke deep into his lungs. He spoke in a squeak to hold it there. "This war, as you call it, is majorly fucked. I guess I got into it because I wanted to show my pa I could defend the US of A as good as he could."

He expelled the smoke and held out the joint to me. I waved it away.

"I was a good GI boy, too. Blasted away at jungle when I saw anything move, tossed grenades into huts if I was told there was Cong in them, that sort of thing. And always returned to my sweet little mama-san at night."

He inhaled again. His pupils swallowed the light of its red glare.

"Then it didn't make sense anymore. The new guys, a lot of blacks, hippie kids, and stuff, they were fragging officers and staying too loose. And the enemy? Shadows."

"So why don't you just turn tail and give yourself up?"

He exhaled. "Can't."

I was getting impatient. The sound of splashing water came from behind the stilt house. Wichai was showering.

When I took a step back, Ben continued. "I know too much."

41

I allowed him his fatalism. "What if you're caught?" I asked. I pictured Wichai spilling water over himself just a few yards away. His damp hair would be dripping in black strands down the nape of his neck. His skin shimmering with only the moon's huge blind eye looking down on him.

The man shrugged his shoulders. "They'll kill me, I reckon. See, I'm special division, in on plans to invade neutral countries, manipulate friendly governments, that sort of thing. They can't rely on me anymore. They'll dump me and enter it as another MIA. Terminate with extreme prejudice, they call it," he said with a laugh. He took another drag. It was almost burning his fingers.

"Why do you want to tell me all this?" I asked.

He looked at me deeply with his mad eyes. "Because I want to trust you, Pete."

"Why?"

Ben threw the butt at his feet and ground it out. "So I won't have to kill you."

A needle of fear jabbed my gut. I think he meant it. The sound of water spilling over the concrete slab stopped. It was totally silent.

"Listen, Ben. I won't tell I saw you here, but not because I fear you. It's just that your affairs are no concern of mine. I have enough on my mind without worrying about you or the war. Actually, I support the war effort, if it's going to stop these people from becoming slaves to Communism. I think we owe it to help our friends."

"Okay, I got your point," he shrugged. "You still think that crap about America the beautiful and all that. That's fine." He seemed to think a moment. "I trust you, Pete. Sorry if I came on like Godzilla. Where I come from, people are not taught to trust anything but their instincts. Mine say you're okay."

I held out my hand and he shook it. "I'm leaving tomorrow, Ben. What are you going to do?" There was a tremor in his grip.

"Got to get out of here," he said with a shake of his head. "Got to get to neutral territory."

He mumbled something I didn't catch and turned to go. I watched the night absorb him.

After a quick shower, I climbed the stairs to the veranda. Wichai's mother set out sleeping mats, side by side, for her son and me. I've wondered since if she was promoting our affection, or if it was merely the most economical and sensible arrangement. Whatever the reason, the boy and I were soon lying beside each other, the events of the day draining from me. The picture of Ben momentarily dominated the foreground, his desperate face mad for some escape from the web he'd found spun around him. Then, I pushed the image away and thought only of Wichai lying at my side.

We had shared many things, the boy and I, but had never slept together. I jumped as he ran his fingers up and down my arm, tickling over the hairs and making them erect. Crickets once again chirped in the forest and a gecko went through its throaty croaking beneath the house. I lay still, loving him so much, feeling both exhilarated and inadequate by that love.

"I have a problem," I choked, looking straight up at the full moon.

"What is it, Ajan Peter?"

I turned my head toward him. His eyes were wide. I raised on one elbow and leaned over him. The youngster didn't move as I lowered my lips to his and kissed him. It is not a Thai gesture, but Wichai's lips responded, working sensuously against mine.

I orgasmed with the kiss! A sweet jolt of heat swelled in the pit of my stomach and burst open. I soaked my pakama in surge after surge of passion.

My lips lifted from his. I sensed that a line had been crossed, that perhaps I had assumed too much. Shame over my body's loss of control engulfed me. I desperately hoped the boy wouldn't hate me for my awkward display of affection.

But he smiled! "That is no problem," he said quietly. "That is a solution."

Wichai's words struck me dumb. He seemed ageless, the phantom lunar light streaking over him through the netting.

43

I saw Ajan Prasit's wise face in the boy's. I couldn't act any more that night. I was exhausted.

Without answering him, I turned away from Wichai, tucking my soggy pakama firmly between my legs. It was long after I heard the boy's even breathing that I found relief from my whirling emotions in a deep and dreamless sleep.

7

The two events that took place that night of Loy Kratong were to determine an unraveling chain of events which would bring me both joy and despair. But I didn't know that as I prepared for the end of the term back at the college, and for a trip to Bangkok during the break. I was going there to work on a project at Thammasat University for the Ministry of Education.

Wiboon was going to move into the dormitory the next term, and earn money by working in the college store for his board. He had grown into a more independent young man during his first few months away from his small village.

Wichai was as devoted and energetic as ever, and expressed more sadness at our separation. It would only be a month, I assured him. We climbed the stairs to Ajan Prasit's house the evening before I left. The campus was already unnaturally quiet as most of the students had returned to their homes.

"Ah, it is good to see you," greeted the Headmaster. His smile, as always, was youthfully warm, yet his eyes beamed with that secret serenity endowed by wisdom.

We sat on his veranda feeling the renewal spirit. There was small talk, what I would teach and what classes Wichai would take. News of families passed back and forth. Then, Ajan Prasit brought the visit to a focus.

"You wish to continue to stay with Ajan Peter, Wichai?" asked the Headmaster.

"Yes, Ajan Prasit. He is my teacher and like a father to me." The boy spoke without reserve, and I again envied his honesty.

The man turned to me. "You wish the boy to continue living with you, Ajan Peter?"

"Yes," I nodded.

"That is good," said Ajan Prasit, as though blessing the arrangement. "The Loy Kratong Festival reminds me of words of the Lord Buddha. 'Thousands of candles can be lighted from a single candle,' he said, 'and the life of the single candle will not be shortened. Happiness never decreases by being shared.' "

There was silence. The boy and the Headmaster had apparently worked this out for my benefit.

Wichai asked, "Ajan Prasit, I have not yet trained as a monk. Forgive me, but please tell me. How does a person know love from lust?"

"Ah, that is both easy and difficult to answer, my son. The Buddha says, 'Of all the worldly passions, lust is the most intense. All other worldly passions seem to follow in its train.' "

I sat stunned by the boy's question, then almost mortified by the Headmaster's answer. But he was not finished.

"That makes the answer seem easy, does it not? But things are never that simple with human emotions, Wichai." He looked from the boy to me. "In a good man, love will enlarge the happiness of both, whether jealous people call it lust or not. You must keep your mind pure, and you will know for yourself."

We left, quiet in our own thoughts.

Wichai and I spent the last night before the break in almost complete silence, he busy cleaning around the house as I read and listened to Prokofiev. It was with regret and, oddly, with a sense of relief, that I left him the next morning for a bus to the train station. I felt I was leaving something of myself, something I both cherished and feared.

8

I won't go into many details of my stay in Bangkok. It was my first extended time in the capital, but it was filled with mindless work revising textbooks and rather typical sight-seeing tours of the city. It was huge and chaotic, so utterly different from the country home in Roi-Et I had grown used to. I felt somewhat out of place.

I missed Wichai.

The cheapest of hotels, really a brothel near the Emerald Buddha Temple, was my home — a simple room for five dollars a day. My room had mirrors on the ceiling and all the carports had large flaps on them to conceal the identity of visitors. It suited my budget and except for the noise peaking the early evening, it was perfect.

I only worked at the university until noon or so, then had the rest of the day to myself. I read some, bused to different sections of Bangkok, walked around, visited shops and bookstores. Some evenings I went to movies with friends working at the university, or we went to dinner and talked late into the night.

It didn't take long for me to get to know the people working at the hotel. They knew I didn't stay there for the pleasure of its women, and were tolerant of my privacy. The hotel had a cafe within its courtyard where I had breakfast in the morning and often lunch at noon when I returned from the university.

I sat there now, alone with my fried rice and iced coffee. I definitely missed Wichai.

A couple boys worked at the hotel, collecting laundry, bussing tables and such. I hardly noticed them at first. Then this day while having lunch, I looked up from my book after lunch and saw the older one, busy washing one of the guest's cars in the courtyard. He worked smoothly and slowly over the shiny metal, wearing shorts and one of those t-shirts with just small straps running over his shoulders. When he lifted his arm to soap over the roof of the car, I saw his hairless armpits gleaming with a sheen of sweat.

The boy saw me staring and smiled. Half of one of his front teeth was chipped off, and it gave him an appealingly roughish look. He had a sensuality to him I didn't see in Wichai, perhaps from the way he moved, perhaps because of the rounded flesh of his arms. He wasn't fat by any means, but he wasn't as thin as Wichai. He smiled again, more playfully, raising his dark brows.

I returned with a tight grin and glanced quickly back down to my book. But I raised my eyes almost immediately, for once letting my feelings guide me, allowing myself to openly watch the graceful boy weave around over the car as he soaped and hosed its shiny surface in the sunshine. He met my eye every so often, and smiled again.

The job over, the boy took the pail and hose and disappeared. I returned to my book, not seeing the words, feeling the blade of desire cutting through me.

I called for another iced coffee. The girl turned and went into the kitchen. A minute later, the boy emerged with my coffee. He set it on the table and stood beside me.

"Thank you," I said, excited by him standing so close. "What is your name?"

"My name is Choochai," he said. "Do you like to look at me?"

"Yes. You are a very handsome boy."

"You are a very handsome man."

We spoke in Thai. I sensed that the boy knew little English. "Do you go to school?" I asked.

48

"No. I just work here to help support my family. We are very poor," he said smiling, and ran his tongue over the space left by his broken tooth.

I more or less ignored his remark. It seemed typical of Thais, I had learned, to say they were poor when speaking with Americans, imagining, I suppose, that we were all rolling in wealth.

Choochai grinned mischievously. "I love you," he said impulsively.

"Do you want to sleep with me?" I asked, just as impulsively.

"No, no, no," he giggled. His eyes and the sway of his wiry body against my arm said *yes*.

I showered and waited in my room that night, trying to read, wondering if I had judged the playful conversation accurately. Was the boy teasing, or would he come after all? I had given him my room number to reinforce the reality of my invitation. Was he just a hustler? Did I care?

Beyond the playful experimentation of my early adolescence, I had never dared surrender to my nature, had never held a boy, hadn't even allowed myself to consider a boy the valid object of my sexual desires. For the first time I had risked declaring my nature. Looking back, I can see how exaggerated I'd made the whole thing, but I never regret my memories of waiting there, anticipating Choochai's knock at my door, determined to let nothing hinder me from pleasure so long denied.

A knock on the door. It was Choochai, eager and nervous. He latched the door and tucked a throw rug under the threshold, ensuring privacy.

I don't remember anything we said, and it isn't important. The boy took a shower, emerging from the bathroom with his hair damp about his skull, a pakama draped about his waist. He sat at the desk and dusted himself with the fragrant powder furnished with the room. I watched, hungry for his youthful beauty, ignorant still of his expectations.

Finally, the boy flicked off the light and lay beside me. We talked briefly. I was aware of his slender body next to mine, drawing me toward it, tempting me with its boyish grace, available, waiting, inviting.

Choochai reached for my hand and laid it on his groin. I felt his erection through the thin cotton of his pakama, throbbing and hard as a rock. "I love you," he repeated.

My fingers loosened the knot at his waist and opened his only garment, revealing his nudity. His young organ was vibrating stiff off his skinny tummy, just a few short hairs dusting his smooth pubes. A drop of lubricant gleamed at its tip. His testicles were small and very tight. Saliva gushed in my mouth and oily fluid pulsed from my own erection. I flung off my pakama and rolled over onto the boy, mashing my lips into his.

I climaxed immediately, flooding out between our rubbing bellies. The boy's tongue worked against my lips and drilled into my mouth as I swam in orgasmic delights. I responded, and our tongues twirled around each other, through the gap between his teeth. Choochai tasted sweet yet rich, innocent yet lusty. Our naked bodies moved together in our sweat and my juices as we kissed deeply.

The boy bucked up against me in urgent spasms. I felt his bone-hard penis rub against mine, then felt the jets of his release mix with mine between our fevered bodies.

I ran my lips down his neck and rested them against his lean shoulder as our energies subsided. I waited for the pang of guilt to hit me.

It didn't.

Instead, wonderfully, I felt a renewed passion well up in me, seeking release. Choochai was ready when I raised up over him. He sighed deeply and spread his legs. He lifted them high over his head and smiled up between his knees. I was harder than ever, gleaming with our natural lubricants. I moved toward the boy and he reached around to guide me into him. He gave just a wince at the thrilling penetration.

I eased in slowly, feeling his moist, hot grip around me. The boy gave me the most incredible sensations I had ever felt. It was more than I could believe possible, and I surrendered to the lust steaming up with us both.

50

"I love you," Choochai repeated as I journeyed through him, not stopping till I nestled firmly into the hairless slit between his firm buttocks. His small penis remained aroused, tapping into his wrinkled tummy.

The boy's words, however meaningless, fired my desires further. I drew out and tunneled back into the youth. The sliding plunge continued, over and over. Nothing else existed but the submissive and responsive boy beneath me, and the enveloping bliss of our sexual union with each other.

My hips bucked erratically, and he lifted his little rump to meet my thrusts, gasping with pleasure. His lips drew back in a gasping sneer and his nostrils flared wide as I worked to greater heights of delight with him.

Quick, fluid hugs of his sphincter around the base of my erection signaled his explosive peak. Spurts of crystal liquid spit up over his heaving chest. He grunted with pleasure at each pulsation. He turned his head and bit into the sheet as he writhed in ecstasy, his arms wide, fingers clutching at the bedding.

I slowed my thrusts, hoping to prolong my own pleasure. But it was futile. Watching the youngster climax with such wild abandon would have been almost enough in itself to take me over the edge of control. But that, and the action of Choochai rippling around my sensitive flesh brought me to the heady oblivion of sexual pleasure. I fell on the boy and filled him with my liquid passion, in long, sweet surges, each one more agonizingly pleasant than the one before.

I remained within Choochai for many minutes as our heartbeats slowed to normal. We parted, and I withdrew. Without words, we showered together, soaping each other with slow, easy strokes. We dried and returned to the bed, still naked. We fell against each other. I was still hungry for the feel of his flesh against mine. He fell asleep first.

The next morning we repeated our performance, this time extending our pleasure for over an hour as I explored his adolescent body.

Choochai had learned the arts of seduction well before our encounter. His own supple beauty needed little to entice a boy lover into his arms. And I knew ours was a union of bodies, not of souls. The boy was intellectually limited, however physically desirable and uninhibited. His emotions were limited to physical pleasure, I knew, and there was nothing noble in what happened between us.

Over the next two weeks of my stay in Bangkok, we tried to duplicate the heady abandon of our first night, and without clear success. The sex became expected, almost mechanical after the first few nights. I indulged the boy in gifts and a little money to enhance his meager salary at the hotel, and I always enjoyed our wild coupling. Choochai withheld nothing, and encouraged me to experiment in our sex, but I missed Wichai's playful humor and bright mind more and more.

I was deeply grateful to Choochai, however. It was with him that I was able to begin shedding my more useless inhibitions, the restraints on my emotions which only served to pervert them into a festering fantasy I could never realize.

9

I had no remorse at leaving Bangkok. I knew that Choochai's easy profession of love would as easily be forgotten, or transferred to another after I left.

When I returned to Roi-Et, there was the activity building to a crescendo beginning the new term. A colleague in the English Department got married the day I arrived, and all the teachers and students who had already returned from leave attended the wedding. I suffered a mammoth hangover the next morning.

As I got my fickle little kerosene burner going in dawn's feeble light, my blurring mind ticked off the memory of what I had said to the new groom the night before: I had offered him and his bride my home!

Not that odd an idea, really. The man, as a bachelor, had lived in a single-room little shack over the student store in the middle of the campus; the house furnished me by the college was two bedrooms large. Because of the whiskey, and because of the guilt that I hadn't got them any other gift, I hadn't even thought of Wichai! Certainly, the two of us couldn't live in that small place together.

As though summoned by my thoughts, the boy's voice came from under the house. "Ajan Peter! It is Wichai! Are you there?"

I went to the veranda and waved. The boy was beaming, more attractive than ever, seeming to almost wiggle about in his joy at seeing me. I felt like a louse, and didn't know how to tell him that he would have to live in the dorm, while I again lived alone.

"I hear we are living over the student store, Ajan Peter!" the boy said, climbing stairs, his satchel swinging from his shoulder. "That will be closer to the school. It is also small. It will be easy to clean."

I shook my head and took the youngster's hand. He had it all worked out, and managed to see the good in the move, as well. I felt immense relief, as well as new interest in what future we might share together.

We moved the next day, commandeering carts from the college and piling up what would fit into the single room. As we were drawing up to the college store, a Toyota came alongside, one I hadn't seen before. I saw the driver was a farang and stopped.

"Go ahead and take these things up, Wichai," I said, approaching the man who got out of the car. He had thin blond hair swept over his scalp, and gas-flame blue eyes. Just from the way he moved, I could tell he was comfortable in Asia. There is a tentativeness, a fear translated into the muscles, of an American who feels out of place here, as though they are stepping on someone's toes.

"You Peter Carpender?" asked the man, wiping his brow with a red handkerchief. He wore a flowery shirt and khaki pants.

"Yes. And you?"

The man extended his hand. "Mark Fisher. I'm with USOM, out of Korat."

"What can I do for you?" I asked. For some reason, the man set me on edge. I figured it was perhaps his direct manner. I was getting used to Thai subtlety, and his American gruffness put me off.

He glanced around, wiping his beady brow again. "Can we get a beer or something around here?"

I ordered iced coffee and led him to a couple wooden chairs set up under the student store. There was some small talk until after the coffee arrived, then he leaned forward earnestly.

54

"I'd like to depend on you, Peter. I'd like to know more about this area."

"Sure, what do you mean?"

His watery blue eyes drilled into mine. "Well, I understand you get out into the villages hereabout, visit families of the students and such."

"Yes."

"Well, I'd like you to be able to share anything, well, unusual, that you might spot on your visits."

"Unusual?" I somehow didn't like this man.

"We have reports of a deserter wandering into one of the provincial villages, Peter. We'd like to get him." Fisher then pursed his lips as though something vital had been settled.

I thought of Ben Ferrall. A shiver ran through me and my spine sprang tight. I had promised to tell no one of his presence. To do so would, I felt, destroy the fragile reality the man held on to. I waited, forcing a neutral gaze on the man.

"Have you seen an American hiding out in one of the villages, Peter, or even heard of someone like that?" asked Mark, licking this thin lips. "Such a man would stand out here like a sore thumb, you know."

A direct question. I felt as though I was standing outside myself, observing how I would face the dilemma. Would I lie, and jeopardize myself with my own government? Or would I tell the truth, and betray the trust of Ben Ferrall? I met Wichai's eyes as he looked down from the small porch of our new home. For some reason, the boy's gentle look focused the issue.

"You're not really with USOM, are you?" I asked, evading Fisher's question. I suspected that he wasn't. The United States Overseas Mission was concerned, in my experience, with aid and assistance. I knew they were the people to contact for the American Field Service, a program I wanted to work with.

"Well, actually, I'm with a division of the agency, Peter.

I freelance for Air America." He jutted out his chin as he said it.

"That's just a front for the CIA, isn't it?" I knew it was. I'd heard stories of Air America planes off-loading rice, only to have one split open on the tarmac, spilling M-16s and grenades. Alarms went off in my brain and I knew I would honor Ben Ferrall's secret.

"Okay, not USOM, Peter," he said without a blink. "But not CIA either."

I knew it was CID then, but I didn't want him to know I knew it. "Then what?"

"Just keep your eyes open," he said, like it was a command.

When Mark Fisher left, I knew he held suspicions. I watched his yellow Toyota pull away, raising a cloud of dust. I knew I would see the man, or others like him, again. I gulped the rest of my iced coffee to get rid of a bad taste in my mouth.

"Ajan Peter!" cried Wichai.

I looked up to the boy.

"Come look. Our home is ready!" he cried, with an eager wave of his hand.

There was only one bed, a wonderful teakwood-framed double bed which dominated the room. A large wardrobe stood along one wall, with a small desk and a bookcase taking up the remainder of the space. It was cozy, and I felt that Wichai and I had established a place of our own, isolated and together in the very heart of the busy campus.

"We should sleep early," I said as we got everything in place through the evening. "The bus will leave at two o'clock."

We were going on a field trip to celebrate the beginning of the term, heading first to Bangkok, then to sections of the South. I offered to chaperon the trip along with two other teachers. Wichai was eager.

"I have never seen the South before," he said, tucking in the sheets on our huge bed. "I have only seen Bangkok in pictures."

I thought of Choochai. We would spend only an afternoon in Bangkok and we wouldn't see each other, not that I
wanted to all that much. I wondered what Wichai would
think of my affair with the boy hustler. I sensed that he would
feel that it was a good education for me, and a profitable
diversion for the boy.

We lay in our new bed, the sounds of the college store
being shuttered up beneath us. An atmosphere of vital tran-
quility surrounded us in the darkness of our new little home.
The only sounds were a repeated three-tuned song coming
from somewhere above us in the night.

"What is that sound?" I asked the boy. "It sounds like
a flute."

"It is a kite, Ajan Peter. The villagers put bamboo pipes
on their kites and fly them in the wind of the cool season.
They think the kite music will keep away evil and please the
spirits of the sky."

The melodic tones were hypnotic. I seemed to be trans-
ported into a trance. Perhaps that's what gave me the courage
to speak. "I love you, Wichai," I said with my eyes fixed
on the ceiling. I had never said anything more honest. I felt
utterly vulnerable, terribly relieved.

It was Wichai who leaned over me this time. His youthful
face was intent, his eyes wet. He kissed me.

I embraced the slender youngster passionately, stripping
off his pakama with a swipe of my hand down his back. I
loosened my own and felt the boy against me for the first
time, without inhibitions.

We were both firmly aroused, eager for sexual pleasure
to enhance our fondness for each other. Our love-making was
charged with irresistible drives, tender and compulsive. His
body was responsive, squirming with passion one moment,
surrendering to my eager caresses the next. It was the culmi-
nation of all our shared moments, peaking out over and over,
each moment more deliciously loving than the last. Our moaning and sighing subsided, only to begin again, with new and
delightfully erotic sensations coursing through us. I was dis-

tantly aware of the fluting kite weaving overhead, blessing our union.

The intensity of Wichai's ardor took me to greater heights than I dreamed of with Choochai. It was the burning of love, unconditional and unafraid, that sparked our arousal and made it infinitely more satisfying. And the boy abandoned himself to my desires just as he threw himself into everything he did.

"You want me like this, Ajan Peter," asked Wichai, and offered himself for penetration. His eyes seemed to beg for it.

But I hesitated. I didn't want to risk hurting the young boy. I didn't think I could have remained hard if I saw his pain. The boy's gesture alone was enough to send renewed power surging through me. I wrapped my lips about his hardness as I felt him twist around beneath me, his hands clawing at my shoulders and down my back. His eager juices soon laced my tongue. The youngster tasted of flavors I could not dream of.

Wichai took me into his mouth. A strangled cry, and I was beyond control, feeling his throat work in gulps and swallows.

Sated and happy beyond words, Wichai and I toweled off and dropped back onto the bed, my arm behind his neck, his fingers tracing over my chest. He twirled the light hairs dusting my nipples. "Ajan Peter is now my dying friend."

"Dying friend?"

"Yes, Ajan Peter. In Thailand we have three kinds of friends: eating friends, playing friends, and dying friends," explained the boy. "I would die for you, Ajan Peter."

Wichai's courage left me speechless.

10

The blaring air horn of the bus just below our window awakened us. Sleepy, but amazingly refreshed, I rushed to get ready for the field trip. Wichai was prepared, watching me with soft eyes as I stuffed my shaving kit into a duffel bag and hitched the strap over my shoulder.

"Ready!" I said.

"Let's go sightseeing!" said the boy.

Wichai sat far back in the bus with his school friends, while I hunkered into a seat in front where the curve of the wheel-well provided a cramped footrest. The other teachers and I chatted, then fell silent as the miles rolled by, the flat country broken somewhat as we descended from the Korat Plateau. Then I dozed, thinking of Wichai, how spontaneous he was, and how delicate I thought our love. I would discover it was stronger than I realized.

Hours passed by in a dreamy hot roar of the engine. The quilted land of paddies gave way to factories, then densely crowded village communities surrounding Bangkok.

The bus, emblazoned with a banner which carried the school's name, blended in and out of Bangkok's chaotic traffic. We stopped only long enough for a visit to the zoo and to eat a bowl of noodles, then headed south.

It was night when we arrived at Prachuab. Wichai and the other students unloaded and entered the teachers' college hosting our visit, and there set up mosquito nets and mats for their beds in the dormitory. With the other teachers, I was shown into rather Spartan quarters which would have intimidated me only a few weeks before. The Prachuab teachers held a banquet for us, and I had my first experience with the flavors of the South.

It was an hour or so before I could get with Wichai.

"Are you all right?" I asked.

"I am fine, Ajan Peter," he smiled.

I had suffered from the irrational fear that the youth might have undergone a traumatic shock from our love-making. I sighed with relief. I still had much to learn.

The boy took my hand. "Ajan Peter, let's go to the beach. I have never seen the ocean before."

Growing up on the West Coast, it never occurred to me that there were those denied the beauty of the seas. How wonderful that the boy's first experience with the ocean would be with me!

"Let's go!" I said, giving his small hand a squeeze.

The evening was kind to the little harbor town. There was hardly a movement in the palm fronds along the curved margin of the bay. It was small, like a miniature Rio de Janeiro, with a high rounded rock looming out of the water on the far side. Stars were intense, like a carpet of shattered crystal, and the half-moon glimmered off the water.

Wichai was at first silent, seeing so much water in one place. His eyes caught everything, sweeping over the water, dazzled by it.

"It is beautiful, Ajan Peter. It is like the earth has a song," he finally said.

I turned my head down to the boy. Where did he come up with such things to say, I wondered, loving him more and more. "Let's go in the water, Wichai."

We slipped into our pakamas under a palm as a couple of villagers walked slowly past, their backs bent and the beams of their flashlights playing over the sandy beach.

"They look for crabs," said Wichai. "They do it along the river when it is low also." He fastened the knot around his waist and headed for the water. "Come, Ajan Peter!" he cried, his feet kicking sand.

The boy flung himself into the water with the same ardor he gave to everything, spreading his thin arms wide and slicing straight through the warm breakers. Droplets of silver flew off his slender silhouette as he frolicked in the darkness. Small, warm breakers hissed around him.

I dove in after him and was bathed with a tepid gel of the gulf. I swam with strong strokes and joined Wichai as he was spouting and slapping around.

It was the most mindless time I'd yet had. With our love declared, I felt a freedom and strength I'd never experienced before. I felt wonderfully reckless and unshackled.

"You are beautiful," I said, smiling at the boy and tossing back my dripping hair.

"I feel beautiful because you think so, Ajan Peter," Wichai grinned, his teeth white in the fluid tropic night.

The boy and I moved a couple yards through the water to each other. Our extended fingers touched, dripping, just above the gentle waves. We reached for each other and held firmly, then kissed. I tasted the child and the warm salt of the sea on his mouth.

Wichai hummed in his throat as he had done before. His pleasure sounds were deeply erotic. I felt his arms drop from around me and lower them to remove his pakama. The boy wanted to make love in the water!

I was hard against him. As he bent, lifting his leg to tie the cloth around his ankle, I did the same. We held each other again, feeling the soft swirl of the water between our legs. Our hands played over each other's shoulders and down backs slick with sea water. I cupped the small, firm mounds at the base of his back in the palms of my hands as he moaned and squirmed against me.

We moved wordlessly to shallower water, where I sank to my knees and pulled the boy onto my lap. In that position, we were eye to eye, man and boy, with the water surging around up to our chests. Wichai had the impish look of a water sprite, naked and wet, an inviting smile on his lax lips. I mashed my mouth against his, more excited than ever in my life by his lean brown body totally surrendered to me there in the surf.

His lips still rubbing against me, Wichai reached between our bellies and guided my hard organ up between his own legs. He raised slightly up off my lap as he centered it, then eased slowly down.

I let him work at his own pace, yet was fighting the compulsion to thrust up my hips, to wedge into his warm, moist body and penetrate him totally, in a single painful plunge!

We both gasped as Wichai nudged down over my crown and I entered him. He threw back his head and winced, baring his teeth like a monkey. Then he lowered further, with steady pressure, over my throbbing erection, and I felt his elastic ring ripple down the length of my shaft.

Wichai worked to take my girth until he squirmed his small buttocks into my groin, totally impaled. I was unprepared for such heat, such gripping moisture enveloping me. Even after my experiences with Choochai, I was breathless with Wichai's wild passion. He seemed to quiver with orgasmic intensity as he stirred my hard sex around within him, nuzzling his lips into my neck as he mumbled and hummed.

My hands explored every curve of his boyish body, my lips running over his slippery skin as I gently rocked him over my lap. The ecstasy was like a hot sob caught at the back of my throat, aching to be cried out! The water churned around us, and we moved with its gentle tug. The orgasmic tides swelled within me as Wichai worked to pleasure me. I became compulsive, wanting him so badly. I bit into his soft lips and nipped at his chin and cheek. My fingers kneaded his firm body, and pulled him to me until I hoped we would melt together as one, so tightly did we hug.

It was impossible to tell if his grunts and groans were signs of pleasure or pain. But we were beyond both, caught in the whirling waters of love about to boil over.

"Wichai, Wichai," I stammered, jabbed into him brutally now, needing release.

"Ah, Ajan Peter!" said the boy, tensing against me.

I felt a rapid series of rippling nips about my root. Wichai was gasping with orgasm. I looked down and saw his pearly juices rise to the surface between us and drift with the push and pull of the water.

That was it! Wrapping him tightly and jerking up into him hard, I peaked. I lived for moments in a timeless, mindless oblivion that was so wonderfully sweet, hot and total.

Our passion ebbed with the water, which now lapped over our bellies as we continued to hold each other. I took Wichai in my hands, around his waist, surprised they almost encircled him, and eased him up off me. He rose up to his feet in front of me, slick from the sea, and I kissed his softening penis, then buried my face in his warm groin.

"We must dress," Wichai whispered. He put his hands to my shoulders and I stood, dizzy and drunk with joy.

We wrapped our wet pakamas around us and headed up the dry sand. When we were dried and dressed, the young boy took my hand. "I don't know of anything beyond dying friend, Ajan Peter," he said. "I could not feel closer to you."

I was never very good at promises, so I was wise enough not to make one to the boy just then. Instead, I responded with something like a lewd joke, but with the best intentions. "I cannot be closer to you than within you, Wichai."

He understood and chose to smile.

11

We stood on the beach, digging our toes into the sand and listening to the hiss of breakers slice over the sand.

"Let's climb to the top," he said eagerly, pointing to the rock rising out into the bay. "There is a temple at the top I heard of in a story."

When we got to the base of the rock there was a loud chattering which made me jump. Then dark, furry little shapes began to emerge around the scattered boulders in the moonlight.

"They are our cousins. See, they are monkeys, Ajan Peter!" yelped Wichai.

Scores of the scampering animals came to life out of the very rock as we approached. I pulled back on Wichai's hand, unsure.

"Come, Ajan Peter," said the boy. "They only bother us if we have bananas."

He was right. After some sniffing and barking, the monkeys settled back into the darkness and we began climbing the steep steps carved out of the stone. I followed him closely, feeling his heat and almost tasting the salty moisture filming his slender limbs.

Florescent lights flickered on in the small pavilion as we reached the peak of the rock. It was like a beacon above the bay, with its steeply sloped roof curling up in graceful nagas, sheltering an image of the Buddha and several folding chairs.

A priest approached from a hut, adjusting his robes and smiling softly.

"Come, come," he said. "Sit. You must be tired from the climb." The man was, like all priests, shaven of hair and eyebrows, his dark eyes serene and curious. He could have been twenty to forty years old.

"Thank you," I said. "The temple is very beautiful."

"Ah, a mere shrine," he said, pulling his chair close. "It has been here for many years, as a symbol of sanctuary for the fishermen." The he grinned wider. "You saw the monkeys?"

"Yes," Wichai and I said together.

"It is said that the shrine will bring luck only as long as the monkeys prosper. So the villagers bring them fruit every day, and more on festival days."

"Do you believe it?" I asked.

The man thought for a moment. "That is difficult to say. But the Lord Buddha has a way of bringing all into harmony, the most devout meditation along with the animal hungers lingering at its base."

The analogy shook me. It seemed that he spoke of my love for Wichai, with its selfless power, living beyond my desires, but fed at its core with my lustful animal energy.

"You have heard of yin and yang?" he asked gently. "The world is entwined, and there is no sense in separating its parts. They are immutably fused. Giving our lives direction is what should concern us, and looking beyond life's illusions."

I was losing him, drifting into his eyes. I was tired, and the air was beginning to cool. My mind was not yet disciplined enough for this discussion, and neither my Thai nor his English could continue much longer. The image of Wichai and me wrapped together, like the yin and yang, stuck in my mind, and we began to spin, going up to the clouds and down to the ground like a yo-yo. I shook my head, clearing it.

"You must be very peaceful here," I said lamely.

"Yes, it is beautiful, isn't it?" For a moment, all three of us were silent, listening to the hiss of the waves below us.

The priest reached down into his monk's bag and drew something out.

"Take this, as a reminder of this shrine," he said, holding his hand out to me.

I would remember this token. It was a reminder not only of this place, but of the night when a new honesty blossomed in me. An honesty nudged free by Wichai and his love for me. I sensed that my new awareness showed in my eyes, they focused so clearly. I took the small votive image of Buddha from him. It was in the Sukhothai style, my favorite, the Buddha smiling the self-assurance of a saint, but his body flowing with the sinuosity of a dancer. Then I raised my eyes, my brows lifted in question.

"You two are very happy together, yes?" he smiled. "It is perhaps like the Tao sign, yin and yang?"

I merely nodded. Then stood.

Wichai waied to the priest, and I followed, then slipped a ten baht note into the service box within the shrine.

"Thank you for talking with us," said the boy.

On the way down, I slipped the image into my pants pocket. Wichai saw this and protested gently.

"No, no, Ajan Peter. You must never put the Lord Buddha image lower than your waist. Put it around your neck on a chain, or in your pocket here," he said, pointing to my shirt.

I did. I wasn't a particularly superstitious man, and it wasn't that I wanted only to please the boy. But the image had become, with its giving, a symbol of our love, and I didn't want to risk hurting that.

We got back to the college and needed a shower. The salt water was still sticky on us, and the shower room was free now that it was late and many of the students were already under their mosquito nets. Wichai and I splashed ourselves with bowls of water, then soaped up like we were brothers, although we looked at each other's bodies boldly in the light of a single, bright bulb.

More importantly, it was another step toward honesty for me. I didn't try to hide the fact that Wichai and I were

66

intimate on a new basis, not from anyone. It was impossible to hide anything in the close community of a village or a college, anyway. But this was different — I no longer denied it to myself. I was facing parts of me I hardly knew existed, able to now because I was shielded by the boy's unconditional love. There was a lightness, a refreshing ability to absorb new experiences, which I hadn't felt for many years. And Wichai was radiant, more beautiful all the time and larger than life, a warm lens through which I could see everything with a clarity clouded earlier by my self-denial and useless fear.

When we returned to Roi-Et, we were tired and dusty from the nine-hour trip from Bangkok. The water tower which used to taunt me now was a beacon of welcome as we rolled into the dusty campus. When I stepped from the bus, I saw the yellow Toyota parked under the tamarind tree beside the college store. Mark Fisher was sitting in the wooden chair he'd sat in before, sipping a beer he'd evidently brought himself.

"Well, back from the big city, eh, Pete?" he said, standing as he spoke.

"What are you doing here?" I was suddenly angry. This man had no right to invade the little world I was building here in Roi-Et, a world made gentle and passionate by Wichai and Ajan Prasit, the world which wasn't large enough to include his self-important rudeness.

"Just checking in, Pete, that's all," he said, sensing my anger. "Hey, listen. This is what the taxpayers expect, you know, people like me to do their job." Then, with a little sneer, "And you."

Wichai came from the bus with the rest of the students, looking from me to Mark, sensing trouble.

"Go take a shower, Wichai," I said. "I will come soon."

When Mark and I were sitting, he began his real business. "This man, Ben Ferrall, we have some leads on him. You seen him lately?"

"No." That was honest. I had only seen him once. I wondered if Ferrall was any more mad than he had been, now that weeks had passed.

Mark leaned forward and wiped his lips. He lowered his voice with a conspiratorial air. "We got to find him, Pete. He knows things that could be dangerous if shared with the wrong people. Know what I mean?"

"No, I don't," I said, standing. "Listen, Mark, I just got back from a long, hot trip and want to shower. I can't help you."

Fisher rose, his face red. "Listen, little goodie-boy. This isn't Boy Scout stuff. I want to find Ferrall." He leaned so close I could smell him. With a shock, I found the smell of his farang sweat repulsive. It was so sickly sweet compared with the soft spicy scent of Wichai. "I can make life a little uncomfortable for you, Peter. You and your little roommate there."

His eyes went up to our room as he said this and a chill ran through me. But I felt safe, with Wichai, with Ajan Prasit, and more and more, with myself. This man — my countryman — was like an outsider now, a foreigner, an invader.

I put out my hand. "Good-bye, Mr. Fisher."

His hand was wet and hot. "We'll see you again, Pete. And let me know if you catch wind of this Ferrall here about. We can't let a barracuda threaten our waters," he winked.

I heard the rumble of the Toyota diminish as I climbed the stairs to be with Wichai.

"That man, he is not your friend," the boy said. He seemed to have the right instincts.

"No, he wants to find the soldier in your village. Do you know if he is still there?"

"No, Ajan, I don't." He frowned slightly as he undid each button of his shirt and let it fall to the bed. "Is it important?"

"I don't know, Wichai." I studied the youngster, his skin gleaming with a thin film of sweat. "But I want to return to Ban Tawat soon. Can we visit your parents soon?"

Wichai unzipped his pants and let them drop. "I would like to. And my parents will be glad to see you. He hooked his thumbs into his shorts and drew them down and off his legs, standing naked, vulnerable, irresistibly desirable.

68

I stripped off my clothes and fell against Wichai's naked warmth on the bed. We made love quickly, intensely, reveling in our sweaty lust. The tenseness of the trip, then the strain of talking with that man, Fisher, drained from me as we writhed in each other's embrace. The boy radiated languid zeal, a wonderful carelessness for his own needs in his hunger to satisfy mine. Perhaps he felt the same way toward me. I don't know, because we didn't speak. We were like rutting animals, and I was wild for his voluptuous adolescence.

Yin and yang were one. At least it seemed so.

We were both urgent, and withheld nothing, until we were sated and slick with jism as well as our sweat.

Yet, somehow, I never felt cleaner in my life. Nor more innocent.

12

It was the cool season. Not briskly cool as I remembered the air feeling in Pacific Northwest springtimes, but certainly a relief from the oppressive heat and stickiness of the rainy season. The mornings were especially crisp, with a delicious haze of smoke hanging over the campus, and curling around the legs of the water tower and our stilt houses. Farmers were burning chaff in their now-barren fields.

"Same, same," Wichai mocked as he pattered up the stairs and into our room. "Duck eggs, sticky rice, and dried beef!" Each morning the boy biked to the little shanty at the gates of the college and bought our breakfast. He put banana leaves down and held up a plastic bag by the rubber band holding it closed. It was swollen fat with black liquid. "And coffee!"

We ate together as the campus stirred to life around us. Our little house was even more crowded; I had brought in a single bed for Wichai. He understood; I still was under the impression that I had to make appearances pass for reality. it didn't inhibit our love-making in the slightest, so he was content to allow me my face-saving gesture. If anything, Wichai was more desirable than ever. In the evenings, we turned on the lamps over our beds and the light bathed the sheer fabric of the netting in a curtain of soft luminescence. I would read, then look over to the boy doing his homework. He would work naked, on top of the sheets, and when he thought I was looking, squirm seductively around over the bed. Even when he seemed absorbed in reading, his chin on his hands, he would flex his firm buttocks, and I lost interest in my book. After several minutes of this, I would be down to the floor next to his bed, raising the mosquito net to crawl in and embrace him till we tired ourselves into sleep.

After breakfast and a morning shower, we dressed and went to the grounds in front of the main buildings for the daily assembly of the college population. The boy melted in with the neat rows of first year students as I stood in a loose group of other teachers, exchanging small talk and smiling at their shivers in the seventy-five degree morning.

Ajan Prasit stood on the podium after the flag was raised and the anthem had been sung. "We are to begin the annual college fair," he said. "I want each department to make a special effort this year, for the fair will also draw money for the temple. I want you to spend the next weekends in preparation for all the displays and performances."

Well, there goes my trip back to Ban Tawatburi. There was some relief in the thought. Ben Farrell was a reminder of the war, of a culture at odds with the gentle life I had here, of a conflict with Mark Fisher and his ilk. The decision made for me, I welcomed the idea of remaining in Roi-Et over the next few weeks.

I poured myself into my work and my contacts with colleagues more than ever before. And effortlessly. Working with my students to develop an English display gave me a chance to find out about them in a way I never could during classes, and I found their lives fascinating. Given the chance, I would have discovered that this was due to Wichai, really. Unselfishly sharing his life with me had opened my vision to his country and its people, allowed me to appreciate the *now* of life in a way I had never previously enjoyed.

Several of the other bachelors among the staff included me in their activities. We would go to Thai boxing matches in town, where the wiry country boys would bow to the four corners of the ring before each bout, propitiating the spirits with their incantations. The brash music and uninhibited be-

havior of the crowd was so different from ordinary Thai behavior. I loved it.

Afterward we would drink coffee or whiskey in the market,
exchanging stories and telling of plans. Often, a trip to one
of the many brothels on the fringe of town was arranged. I
went a couple times, slightly tipsy. The house was strung
with colored lights like it was Christmas.

"You like her?" said one of my colleagues as a girl planted
herself in my lap.

"Not pretty like American girl," scoffed another.

I didn't know what to do with my hands, so I folded
them loosely around her tightly-wrapped waist.

Well, I gave it a go in one of the rooms, and the girl did
her best to arouse me. But I hardly hoped to prove anything
to anyone. Pleading too much whiskey, I excused myself after
giving her a couple hundred baht. She took it with a kiss.

Wichai, too, enjoyed his own life on campus. He had his
own circle of friends, his morning soccer practice, and his
photography club after school. And his own sense of humor.

The word reached me after lunch one day that Wichai
had broken his arm.

"I saw him with a sling, like so," said a fourth-year student, cradling his arm close to his chest.

Others told me the same story, and I dismissed my class
early to find him. It was the first time worry had been a
part of our friendship; I was desperate to find him. He needed
me now, I thought, as I biked around the college grounds
following leads.

Then I saw him, strolling from the wood shop. His arm
was indeed in a sling. He saw me pedaling up and brightened
into a smile.

"What are you doing here, Ajan Peter?" he asked.

I let the bike fall to its side and went to him. "I heard
you are hurt. What happened?"

"Oh, this?" he said, and lifted his arm from the sling.
"I did this as a joke."

Relief and anger rushed together. And I felt like the boy had made a fool of me. So many had seen my desperate concern.

"I'm sorry, Ajan Peter," he said, as he hung his head.

When I cooled enough to forgive him, he suggested that next time he would never fool me again. Next time his arm would truly be broken.

"Let's have a booth showing pictures of Gemini Space-craft and Atlas rockets," suggested one student.

"We could see American food — hot dogs and hamburgers!" said another.

"Or show holidays in America like Christmas," smiled a pretty girl, one of my favorites.

I sat around the table in the little gazebo near the college gate, surrounded with my fourth-year students, discussing the English Club's project for the fair. Piles of *somtam* and sticky rice disappeared as we talked. *Somtam* — how I used to detest the mouth-burning combination of papaya rind, fermented fish, and hot pepper! Now it seemed as ordinary a snack as potato chips.

Wichai spoke. "We should have something the visitors can participate in if they know any English. Maybe a game."

It was a good idea. But no better than the others. Wichai saying it, however, seemed to move his peers to his as the dominant suggestion. As the boy sat, pushing a handful of somtam and sticky rice into his mouth, the others nodded with unanimous agreement.

I wondered if this was because Wichai was my lover. Did that give his words the added weight of my unspoken approval? Thais had often told me of the great karma I had, as a foreigner who had traveled much and as a professor in the college. Did my lover share my karma, or add to his through our love?

The thought delighted and troubled me at the same time. I scooted closer to Wichai as the decision was reached, the students smiling and ordering more food. Wichai leaned toward me as our legs touched under the table.

"We will make Scrabble boards, Ajan Peter," he said. "You must help us all learn the best words for the game."

"All words are good, Wichai," I said.

The boy swallowed, then grinned in that devilish way of his. "Then you must teach us all words!"

Ajan Prasit heard our laughter as he walked through the gate. His old dog, Joe, was with him as the man took his afternoon stroll from his office to the temple. I remember when the man first told me the dog's name. It seems that Thais often give their animals American names, and he thought I would be offended. His relief turned to mirth when he found I would not take it personally.

The students all waied deeply as the Headmaster approached.

"As you were, my students," he said with a wave of his hand. "Planning for the festival, or are you having a somtam-eating contest?"

"It is the festival, Ajan Prasit," Wichai answered. "Do you know how to play Scrabble?"

The old man's grey eyes danced. "Scrabble? Making up English words? Yes, I've played a little. I had a teacher when I was learning English—I was much older than you students—who used the game when I got bored with my lessons."

"We plan to use the game for the English project," Wichai said. "We will make several boards, and many little letter blocks."

The Headmaster nodded. "Good. There should be joy in learning." He scanned the faces of the students, acknowledging each of them and their importance. When he came to me, his eyes remained and he said, "Ajan Peter, can you come with me to the temple?"

I left my students and Wichai with some final words of preparation, then joined the Headmaster in a slow gait along the dusty path.

"Your future is longer than mine," he said after a few minutes silence.

Future? He saw my confusion. "Look," he said, pointing his cane to our long shadows stretching out and up from our dusty feet over the reddish road. "Our futures run pell-mell out before us, only half seen and without any substance. And yours is longer than mine."

There was a time, I thought, when I would have said, yes, that's because I'm taller. But I was slowly and effortlessly allowing my mind to lose the tyranny of logic which had governed it (with moderate success) for all my years before coming to Thailand. I was learning to accept truths which may have once sounded paradoxical. There was no way of explaining it now.

"Your future, Ajan Peter. Do you think about it much?" he asked gently.

"Much less than I used to," I answered. "I used to mark the calender to see the days remaining before I could go home. Now I am beginning to feel that this is my home."

There was silence for a moment, broken by the buzzings of insects stirring airborne in their evening pursuits.

"I don't think this will ever be your home," the man said. "I have seen many foreigners come, English, American, Japanese, and Chinese. All stay for a while as our guests. But in the end they all return to their homelands, taking a part of us with them and leaving a part of themselves here. But they all leave."

I didn't like the way this was going. I preferred not to think of the future at the moment. Nor of leaving Wichai. "I'm so happy right now, Ajan Prasit. I don't like to think of going home until the time comes."

We rounded a corner of the road and could see the unfinished roof of the temple shining red and green between palm fronds in the oblique light of the setting sun.

"Buddha says, 'Times of luxury do not last long, but pass away very quickly; nothing in this world can be long enjoyed.' Have you thought about the boy?"

My mouth went dry. I really hadn't. I lived as though things would always be as they were. And if I returned home, then Wichai would continue . . . how? "Wichai will complete his education and become a teacher. It is what he wants."

We now stood on the temple grounds. A rosy light bathed its pure white walls. A star or two twinkled in the cobalt sky. Ajan Prasit sighed, then looked up to me. "Do not dwell on it now. But you and Wichai share a destiny. Your shadows have intertwined and can never be separated. Buddha says, 'People favor themselves and neglect others. People let their own desires run into greed and lust. Because of these they must suffer endlessly.' Think if what your shadow, and his, is to become, Ajan Peter."

"Am I unfair, Ajan Prasit, to want to be happy?"

"No," he said softly, leading me on a tour around the temple building. His eyes caught every detail of the work, now largely shrouded in darkness. "You are merely human. I just want you to think of the future, that neither you nor the boy are hurt."

"You seem to know what is in my heart before I do," I said.

"I do."

We stood still. I could see tiny dots of starlight in his eyes. "I once loved as you do, Peter."

It was the first time he had addressed me without the formal title. I wanted to ask more, but the man's weight of office and — karma? — formed a barrier against my curiosity.

"Yes," he said, once again reading my thoughts, "I loved a boy, and it isn't as uncommon as you have apparently been led to believe. With me it was as a monk, when denied the pleasure of women in order to concentrate on the discipline of the temple. I had a novice, a young boy from my home province, to attend to me. We rose before sunrise to gather offerings in the town, he served me our noon meal and we ate together, we sat side by side during chants. And the long evenings were made welcome by his happy presence."

"You — you were. . . ."

"Yes, we were in many ways wedded to each other in the service of the Lord Buddha, during my months of monk-hood. It was a union I shall always cherish, along with the memory of my departed wife."

Ajan Prasit lead me to a low stone bench facing the temple where we sat in silence for several moments. This was a surprise. And it disturbed and comforted me at the same time. Disturbed because I felt what Wichai and I had was unique, and resented the fact that such a love was shared by others. What ego! At the same time I was relieved to know that there was more understanding of what we had than I'd dared hope.

I looked to the temple, now like a ghost against the dark sky. "Do you still see him?" I asked.

"Oh, yes," said Ajan Prasit. "He is now a priest in the province of Songkla, and we see each other occasionally, now as brothers. His priestly name is Pra Anan. I expect him to preside over the dedication of this temple when it is time."

"Did *you* hurt each other, Ajan?"

"Lovers always hurt each other. Perhaps the greatest freedom is our knowledge that man is born alone and dies alone."

Though I waited, the Headmaster said no more. "Thank you, Ajan Prasit."

After an intake of breath, he continued, "There will be a celebration for the halfway point in construction of the temple. We will have an auction for the *cho faa*, and I want you to go to Bangkok during the break and escort a patron back here for me. And I want you to take Wichai with you."

He explained. The cho faa was the snake-like projection out the front of the temple. It signified a spirit-bird, one which unites the earth with the heavens. Some say it is the cobra which, spreading his hood, protected the Lord Buddha as he meditated upon his death. When a temple is half-built, funds are raised for its completion by an auction of wealthy citizens, each eager to earn much merit, and not upset with the news of their reputations enhanced by their generosity. The high bidder was allowed to etch his name at the base of the cho faa, which was then raised to its prominent position, at its topmost peak, to become forever part of the holy build-

77

ing. No temple is complete before the cho faa is properly in place.

I told Wichai that evening.

"Ajan Peter! I have never really seen Bangkok, the temples and the palace! Will we stay there long? What should I take? Are the temples as beautiful as the pictures?"

And other eager questions. My love for him ached within me when he was so boyishly delighted. "First the festival, Wichai, then Bangkok. I think you can teach me more about it than I can teach you."

That night, as we prepared for bed, I wondered about Ajan Prasit, what he had felt and done when he served as a monk. It made me want to be more mature and tender toward Wichai, knowing that years from now we may look into each others eyes; I wanted to be sure that what I saw in Wichai's eyes would not betray my selfishness.

I noticed that the boy moved stiffly as he pulled off his clothes.

"Are you sore?" I asked.

He rubbed his muscles. "I helped move pieces of wood from the carpenter's shop this afternoon. We will need much for our display."

"Lie on the bed, Wichai, and I'll give you a massage."

He flopped belly-down and spread his arms and legs. I got over him, my knees hugging his thighs, and coated my hands with lotion from my medical kit. "This will make you feel better," I said as my hands touched his warm, smooth back.

The boy moaned sensuously as I rubbed him. I ran my hands along his sides, feeling his ribs ripple under my fingers. His shoulder blades looked like angel's wings. I looked at his face, cheek down against the pillow. His black hair spilled over his forehead in careless tresses. His lips were slack and moist, the corners pulling up with pleasure as I felt him in sensitive places, moving at will all over his smooth body. He seemed to glow with a beauty made only more precious by his ignorance of it.

78

Oddly—because he was so precious to me—Wichai thought he was quite ordinary, made special only by my love for him. "I am so lucky to be a Thai boy with such a wonderful friend," he would say.

I moved to sit beside him on the bed and massaged his thighs and tight calves. My fingers pressed into the soles of his feet and searched between each of his little toes. Wichai giggled softly but did not move.

I worked up the fine columns of his legs, and again straddled his legs. My hands trembled slightly as I cupped his firm buttocks in my hands, running my thumbs into the heat of the crease slicing his firm mounds. He spread his legs further. I reached for the lotion and dripped the slick liquid into the warm wrinkle of boyhood winking up at me.

Slowly, like a hydraulic pump driven by a furnace of sweetly restrained force, I lowered to cover him. There was a gasp of pleasure as I entered him, from one or both of us, I can't be sure. Then, bonded together, we slid together into a realm of surging pleasure.

13

Ajan Prasit blessed our trip over breakfast at his house. Afterwards, Wichai and I rode the bus to the train station at Banpai. We got second class seats for Bangkok and settled in for the nine-hour trip. The passing scenery had a zesty color I had never truly been aware of before. Never had the water buffalo moved so gracefully. And never had the farmers in the fields we passed been more attractive. And the rice paddies were green, an intense green, like apple-green jade.

When we stopped in Korat, we bought a bunch of rambutan, sticky rice, and roast chicken. We ordered soft drinks and ate off the banana leaves that served as wrappings.

The train clicked on through the heat of the afternoon, and Wichai moved beside me on the bench seat.

"I'm excited, Ajan Peter, but sleepy," he said. He rested his head on my shoulder and closed his eyes. When his breathing deepened, I too closed my eyes and let the rhythm of the rails lull me into sleep.

We were both awake for the clamorous arrival into Bangkok. Wichai was wide-eyed with wonder. Bangkok is the center of the nation for Thais in a way that Washington is not for modern Americans. Here is the Royal Family, the seat of government, the Buddhist hierarchy and, above all, the opportunity to make it big in a way never possible in the provinces. The ratio of population between Bangkok and the next most populous city, Chiengmai, is the greatest of any country.

That crowded mass of population had produced immense wealth, evidenced in skyscrapers and Mercedes limousines; it had also spawned obvious poverty. Rows of shanties lined the train tracks, and squalor overshadowed the once idyllic canals.

"Is it far to the hotel?" asked Wichai as we walked out from the station. The shoulder bag he carried was light—just a change of clothes and some books. The words 'Pan Am' were printed in large letters on the small bag.

"We'll get a *samla*, Wichai," I said as I looked around for the line of them. "Over there."

A samla is a three-wheeled vehicle, essentially a motor scooter with a thyroid condition, a covered carriage big enough for three or four Thais and one average American. Its unmuffled motor gives it the name it commonly goes by: 'took-took.' We careened through the evening traffic to a government hostel where we would stay courtesy of the Ministry of Education. The patron Ajan Prasit wanted us to escort back to Roi-Et was a deputy minister there.

I watched Wichai as he watched the passing scene. I sensed that seeing the city through his eyes would make it all new and wonderful again. I looked at him closely. His body was alert yet relaxed, close to mine. And I became aware of his smell. I remembered how I'd first filled my nostrils with the scent of the boy as we biked to the market when he first came to live with me. Now, it seemed a more sensual spice cooked off him.

Although I'd been close to him for months, I only now discriminated his scent as distinct from the cascading odors of Bangkok. Perhaps it was because the long trip had allowed Wichai's body to cook off what ordinarily was washed away by his afternoon shower.

I leaned closer, till my nose almost brushed his shoulder. It was an aphrodisiac! It was like opening a cedar chest filled with warm clover and sage. But with an undercurrent of musk that had my heart speeding. He was a beacon drawing my lust, just as he sat there looking away, in his own world.

We showered together at the hostel. After pouring bowls of cool water over each, we lathered and embraced. I drove my tongue between his teeth, tasting him deeply. His flavor was as delicious as his scent. Slick and salty, it now had an evil innocence that hit a hot nerve at the back of my throat. I drove against his belly as he writhed against me. Soapy suds squished between us. Soon, we were panting, holding each other, as our semen oozed down our legs.

Aside from Wichai, two things occupied my thoughts the next day: our mission for the temple and Choochai. The first was easiest to deal with. We'd arrived a day early for sight-seeing and could wait to go to the Ministry.

The second — Choochai — was more disturbing. I'd hardly thought of the boy I'd first had sex with at the cheap hotel so many months before. My love for Wichai had dominated my life so completely, I hardly gave any other boy more than a look.

But I wanted to see Choochai. A desire to have the illicit, perhaps violent sex with the hustler, I suppose. Whatever it was, I couldn't help wondering how I could leave Wichai for a couple hours and give it a try.

"There are so many things I want to see, Ajan Peter," said Wichai as we sat having a breakfast of rice porridge.

"We don't have much time," I said, thinking of planning a couple hours in the evening. "What do you want to see most?"

"Oh, that's easy. I want to see the Emerald Buddha Temple."

Perhaps it was the heady atmosphere of Bangkok that had me thinking about Choochai. There was no good reason to desire him, with a boy I truly loved at my side. Is man by nature perverse? I wondered as my mind dwelled on the times Choochai and I had coupled in my awakening days. Am I drawn toward a promiscuity which defies all logic? Perhaps it was all those years of denial and restraint which, now unleashed, led me to encounter as many and as much of my sexual nature as opportunity offered. And yet, there were opportunities for that with other students which I'd easily declined.

I pushed the idea of arranging a tryst with the hustler out of my mind and concentrated on sharing the day with Wichai. We squeezed onto a bus for the Emerald Buddha Temple. I was unprepared for the spectacle which awaited us as we stepped through the narrow gates and entered the phantasmagoria at the center of the spirit of Thailand.

"The *yaks* guard the temple against evil," said Wichai, looking up at the malevolent stone giants standing at attention on either side of the gate.

We looked beyond these, into the temple grounds. A barrage of colors assaulted us. They were further intensified, these brilliant greens, yellows, and reds, as they were mirrored by the reflecting mosaics covering each pillar and wall around us. It was perfect. Ordinarily, such a display would seem garishly ornate; but here it was apt, a wildly exotic explosion of art in celebration of a people's devotion to the Royal Family and their Lord Buddha.

"Let's get some flowers to put on the altar, Ajan Peter," said the boy.

With lotus blossoms, candles, incense, and a package of gold leaf, we circled the main temple. In front was the altar, a compound surrounding bowls, candle holders, and statues, wreathed in pungent smoke and shimmering with gold.

"It is another way to make merit," explained Wichai as he held out the candles and incense for me to light. "The candle provides light for the spirit, the incense purifies the air. The lotus is a symbol of Buddhism. As it grows from darkness and mud to rise above the water into sunshine, so can souls rise above worldly desires and shine in the light of reason."

Who was the teacher now? And who the student?

I opened the packet of gold. There were ten waxy sheets of paper, each with a square of gold leaf hammered to an almost transparent thinness stuck in the middle. Each was about the size of a postage stamp. "Where do we put these?" I asked.

Wichai peeled a sheet from the pack and leaned over the rail as he pressed the gold, so thin it was almost liquid, onto the forehead of a Buddha. "You put it where you wish the spirit to dwell stronger within you, Ajan Peter. I wish to have a better brain for remembering things from books, so I put it there."

I applied one square to the same place, right over his. I rubbed another over the region of the heart.

At that moment the resonant chorus of monks within the temple began their chant. Unseen behind the walls and altar within, they began their daily anonymous litany of Pali precepts. The compelling chanting resonated throughout the temple complex, wrapping the area in its magical music.

Removing our shoes, we entered the building and sat crosslegged on the highly polished floor. Fans turned slowly overhead and the sweet smell of jasmine scented the air. I followed Wichai in bowing till my forehead touched the floor three times.

We looked at the Emerald Buddha itself, almost lost in the huge cluttered altar. Its green color helped to set it apart. It was delicate, translucent — the most precious of all Buddhas because it was the King's personal patron. Perhaps jasper rather than emerald as I had heard, it was no less special because of that.

As we sat there for several minutes, the chanting seeming to vibrate in my bones, it seemed I felt Ajan Prasit's spirit in the place. I had identified Buddhism with him so strongly, I'd forgotten that I lived in a nation of Buddhists, most simply not as devout nor as learned as the Headmaster. But the spirit of that Indian philosopher born over twenty-five hundred years ago left these people with a gentle fatalism I was just beginning to appreciate.

I leaned down to Wichai, speaking in hushed tones. "It's beautiful. So different from the Christian shouting and yelling I grew up with."

The boy merely looked at me with curiosity.

I continued, "We are taught that all pleasure is sinful,

Wichai. If we didn't do God's will, we would burn in hell for all eternity."

"The priest in our village told us about different religions," he said. "He told us that Christianity is the religion of faith; Islam is the religion of obedience; and Buddhism is the religion of intelligence." Then Wichai grinned, "But he was a Buddhist."

We toured the remainder of the buildings within the compound, including the Chakri Pantheon. This gem-like building is the repository for the remains of the monarchs in the Chakri dynasty, the one which has ruled Thailand since the founding of Bangkok just over two hundred years ago. The former capital was Ayuttya, about sixty miles up the Chao Phrya River, its ruins a site I wished to visit.

When a brutal siege by the Burmese succeeded in defeating that beautiful city, Taksin, a military leader, ventured south to establish a new capital at Thonburi. The man went mad after becoming King, but his capital flourished. Across the river lay the sleepy little village of Bangkok, which was soon absorbed into the growing city, and its name stuck with most of the world. The Thais call their capital Krung Thep —"City of Angels."

Wichai filled me in on this history as we had a lunch of noodles in a small shop. "We should visit Wat Aroon next," he said. "It is where King Taksin founded his new city."

"Is there anything you don't like about Bangkok?"

He thought for a moment. He ran his tongue around in his cheek when he did that. "It is too noisy. And there are poor people. They come from the country because they think they will get rich, but they live in poor houses that don't have water or electricity."

"Why don't they just move back?"

"They sometimes sell their farms. I hope that education will help them. That is one reason I want to be a teacher — to help my country."

And I wanted to be a teacher to avoid the draft! "Does the King worry about poor people?" I asked.

Wichai looked appalled that I would question such a thing. "Oh, yes. He goes to many poor areas and helps them. Ajan Peter, the King is like a god."

"Sometimes I think Thai people treat me like a god, and it isn't very comfortable," I said gently. "It is hard to act perfect."

The boy nodded. "Yes, I am learning that you are just a man." He slurped up the last of his noodles, whipping them between his sucking teeth. "But you are a wonderful man for me!"

"Let's go to Wat Aroon."

We walked the short distance to the river and waited for a water taxi. The rushing traffic of morning had ebbed, but there was a steady stream of boats, large and small, moving through the warm, heavy waters. Long lines of sampans, tethered together and pulled by a barge, rode high in the water as they returned empty back upriver. Those heading to market were so packed with produce that water lapped over their decks.

"Look at the temple, Ajan Peter," Wichai said. "It seems covered with jewels, yes?"

As the water taxi plowed through the water, I looked at the gleaming spire and had to agree.

"Wait till we get close," he said. "I think you will be surprised."

I was. When we got to the base of the great *prang*, the rounded spire, I saw that the whole of it was embedded with china: plates, cups, and saucers. Some were rather plain, but most had colorful designs, all cemented into the body of the temple. Broken wedges flared around the edges, and single droplets of red or green porcelain punctuated a flaring motif.

"Much of this was donated by the people to complete the temple," Wichai explained.

We climbed the steep stairs which reached halfway up the spire, one of the tallest religious structures in the country. From the platform, we had a panoramic view of the river, with the cities of Bangkok and Thonburi sprawling out from it to the horizon. We could feel the wind blow up here.

I felt on top of the world. Wichai and I both were awed by the sight which seemed like a fantasy spread out below us. We stood next to each other pointing out various land-marks, while other visitors chatted and took pictures around us. I put my arm around him and pulled him close. He molded to my side with ease. It was the first time I'd demonstrated our affection in public. Then I wondered what others would think of my unconscious gesture. Tearing my eyes from the scene below, I looked around at the people on the platform.

Not sure of what to expect, I was surprised to find most of them oblivious to our close embrace. Those who noticed, smiled. I hugged Wichai tighter and forgot my fears.

After more sight-seeing, we did a little shopping along Silom Road, a boulevard which serves as the center of shops and hotels catering to tourists. Wichai bought me a holder and chain for the image of Buddha given to me by the priest in Prachuab. We went to a bookstore where I bought books for each of us. He liked some shirts he saw in the window of a department store; I got him two and a new pair of pants.

We were now tired and dirty. We returned to the hostel for a shower and a nap. I woke before Wichai and lay won-dering about Choochai. There was a compulsion to see the attractive little hustler I couldn't deny. I decided to go that evening.

Wichai happily accepted my reasons for leaving him alone for the evening. I told him I wanted to go out to a few bars, perhaps talk with some fellow Americans for a change. He said he could read the little book I bought him.

It was the first time I'd lied to him, in fact the first time I'd lied at all for a long time. It didn't bother me as much as the larger deception of going to meet Choochai.

There was no sign of the hustler as I checked in at the hotel. And there was no sign of interest, either, as I told them I'd only stay a couple hours. When I asked about Choochai, however, there was interest.

"Ah, yes, you desire the boy for the evening?" asked the big Chinese woman behind the desk.

"Yes."

She handed me my key with a flabby hand. "You go to your room. Choochai will be there in maybe thirty minutes, okay?"

It seemed the kid was no longer freelancing. Or perhaps the staff just knew of our earlier liaison. The longer I lived in Thai society, the less surprised I became at the public knowledge people had of private affairs. So far this revelation was convenient, for it served to diminish my guilt over the duplicity involved in achieving my little tryst.

Within an hour there was a knock at my door. Choochai fell into my arms with an ardor that almost knocked the breath out of me. We kissed, and the boy was as energetic in swirling his tongue deep within my mouth as he was in yanking the shirt up from my pants.

The boy wasn't late for lack of passion. He smelled fresh, and I guessed he'd taken the time to shower, as had I. With only the minimal words passing between us —"How long will you stay . . . I love you . . . Take your clothes off"— we were writhing together naked on the bed. The kid was impulsive, his grin of pleasure revealing that broken tooth of his. He held me tightly as we kissed and felt each other over.

Then the heady ride of sexual satiation began. I peaked, then the boy, and we relaxed as I smoked a cigarette. Then again. And yet again.

It was almost midnight when I fell back against the pillow and ran my hand down my chest, finding it slick with our sweat.

I waited for the guilt to hit me again, as I did the first time I'd allowed myself unrestrained lovemaking with the hustler. Again, it didn't hit. Not guilt exactly, anyway. There was a gnawing regret that I'd deceived Wichai. I knew and felt that Wichai could offer me something Choochai simply could not.

Well, I'd found out something. Sex with Choochai was just that. This evening confirmed that Wichai and I had established roots going much deeper, and with more promise for that future Ajan Prasit had talked about. Someday I might even tell Wichai about this. But then, who knows? He would probably know it without my confession.

I stuffed out the cigarette. "I'm going to shower, Choochai. Then I must go."

"No," he demanded. "Stay here with Choochai. I can make you happy many more time, then again in the morning." His large, dark eyes burned with eager pleading. The intensity of his protests irritated me.

"I must go," I said finally, and watched his handsome face fall in disappointment.

"You will come back to see Choochai soon?" he asked quietly.

I assured him I would and he brightened. It was too late and I was too tired to take a bus and afforded myself the luxury of a taxi back to the hostel. As I rode, I found myself wrestling with new self-awareness. I didn't crave sex alone, and Choochai's possessiveness turned me off; I was happy to find that my nature did indeed seek something more noble that a quick tussle in the bunk.

There was a single light burning in the hostel room when I tiptoed in to find Wichai fast asleep in bed. His book lay open and his face was down on the sheet beside it. There was a feeling that parents must get on seeing their child asleep as I looked at him. Vulnerable slumber seemed to endow him with an angelic quality.

I undressed and rolled into bed beside him, then leaned up over him to study his face. It reminded me of something I'd seen recently, the subtle smile of intelligent peace, the closed eyes, the smooth serenity of the boy. What was it?

Then it hit me. In Wichai's was the face of the Buddha.

14

Next day we arrived at the Ministry of Education to inform Ajan Kularb we were ready to escort her back to Roi-Et for the temple ceremony. Ajan Prasit said there would be other wealthy patrons at the auction, but that he pinned his hopes on Kularb for the high bid. Kularb means 'rose' in Thai, and I thought the name a good omen.

It wasn't, at least not at first. The charming, middle-aged woman greeted us pleasantly enough, and I put on my best manners. She doted on Wichai, who seemed to bring out the best in everyone. But as soon as we had exchanged small talk, she walked us to an office, asked us to sit, and told us that a man, an American, wished to speak with us before we left. She returned to her own desk, leaving us alone.

After a moment, Mark Fisher entered the room. He acknowledged us with a perfunctory jerk of his swept, blond head, then sat facing us behind the desk.

"Well," he drawled after a long pause, "I hope you and your young friend are enjoying your visit to Bangkok."

The sarcasm was thick. He said 'young friend' in a patronizingly superior fashion.

"Yes, we are," I answered simply. "Aren't you a little out of your element, Fisher. What are you doing in the Ministry of Education?"

"One hand washes the other, Pete," he said with an arching, innocent shrug of his shoulders. "When I heard you were paying a visit here, I couldn't allow the opportunity for us to chat again pass by."

Then he turned to Wichai. "When did you visit Bantawat last?"

I sensed an imperceptible quiver shake the boy, but he appeared calm in the face of Fisher's barking question. "Once I went there since Loy Kratong Festival. To visit my family and pay my respects."

"Of course," intoned the man. "And you saw your friend Ben Ferrall there when you went?"

Wichai answered without hesitation. "He is not my friend."

I didn't like this man interrogating Wichai. "Why not just ask me the questions, Fisher," I said.

He didn't even turn to look. "I'll get to you, Pete. Now Wichai, this is important. Did you see Ben Ferrall on your last visit?"

I sensed that the boy didn't know how to answer. Innately honest, he knew how I resisted revealing information to this man. His dilemma resulted in silence.

Mark Fisher leaned forward on his elbows, his eyes drilling into the boy. "This is very important, Wichai, not some schoolboy's game. This man has information which could hurt people if he told the other side. You may save lives by your answer."

Wichai turned his eyes to me. I heard the man cluck his tongue as I looked at the boy's eyes. They looked like those of a trapped animal. I had to do something.

"Listen, Fisher," I blurted, "you have no right to question a Thai citizen. Ferrall's your problem. Why don't you solve it yourself."

"You listen. Perhaps you don't realize it, but this man is dangerous. His psychiatric profile was displaying a significant and progressive anomaly at his last session before his desertion. We would have had to pull him in anyway. Just a matter of time. We're here to win a war, buddy, and it's men like Ferrall who can muck it up."

"And perhaps you don't realize it, but I support the war. I don't want to see these people under the yoke of Communism any more than you do. I just don't think we're going about it in the right way."

My agreement to his principles seemed to take some of the wind out of Fisher's sails. His long, thin fingers relaxed and his blue eyes took on some depth. "I got a wife and two kids back in the States, Pete. I know there's opposition to the war, hippie freaks and politicians running for office, that sort of thing." He frowned as though he had a pain. "I didn't realize how bad it was until my wife wrote me last week. She was asking some of the same questions herself. My wife, for god's sake! She knows I'm in this for the career."

Wichai and I remained silent, hoping this was soon over. But Fisher seemed to be started on something he needed to get out of his system.

"Ferrall isn't the only one, Pete. There's scores of them out there, and the CID has me running after them all. The rats are loose. The can ruin it for us all."

"Is Ferrall a traitor?" I asked. It might change things for me — loyalty to country before loyalty to a single individual. I didn't know that one until I had his answer.

"Not yet he isn't," the blond man said with a fist to the table. "At least, not according to my information. But he's dangerous."

"So is the war," I said. "What happens if you find him?" I knew what Ben had meant when he said 'terminate with extreme prejudice.'

"*When* we find him, Pete," Fisher said with a wince. "We'll have to debrief him thoroughly."

"Will you kill him?"

Unruffled, the man rose and turned to face the window behind the desk, his fingers entwined behind his back. When he spoke again, there was a malevolence in his tone that chilled me. "Maybe you want to protect this man Ferrall, Wichai. Maybe you know a good thing when you have it and don't want to give it up. Maybe you're smarter than I thought."

He turned slowly and gazed again at Wichai, suddenly cruel. "Maybe Ben Ferrall is getting into your sweet little boyass just as much as this guy, and you like it too much to give it up."

Wichai gasped, his fingers tight on the arms of the chair. I was appalled. Anger exploded through my chest, then tightened every nerve of my body.

But before I could do or say anything, the man continued. "You getting paid off by two sugar-daddies, is that it? Does Ferrall buy you presents every time he screws your tan Thai tail? You know, real men are getting killed in Nam fighting a war so you faggots can sit back and screw around as you please."

I pushed myself out of the chair, ready to attack Fisher. I wanted to scream at the man, to wrap my fingers around his throat and choke down every rotten word he was saying. I felt Wichai's restraining hand on my arm. I glanced down at the boy, hardly seeing him for the anger hot in my eyes.

"No, Ajan Peter," the boy said calmly. "I think he wants to make you mad, so that your words will lack restraint." Then, quietly, he added, "He is not worthy of hearing your words without your reason."

His words sent the cool rush of control back into me. He also adroitly succeeded in exasperating the CIA man. I fought down the bile Fisher's words had raised and sat back in my chair. What Wichai said made sense, and I had new respect for him. Not only for the maturity and intelligence to recognize the ploy, but for his courage to tell me in front of the man.

I lit a cigarette and inhaled deeply. "You're right, Wichai," I said. "Thank you." Then I turned to Fisher and raised my eyebrows in an arch. "Is there anything more you wish, Mr. Fisher?" I asked, with as much sarcasm as he had employed with us.

It was Fisher's turn to be frustrated. He slapped both hands flat on the desk and looked from one of us to the other. "Get out of here, both of you," he said.

But as we reached the door, he added, "I'll see you again, Pete old boy. Take care."

My eyes drilled darts into Ajan Kularb as we approached her desk. "Why did you let that man see us? We came here at Ajan Prasit's request to escort you back to Roi-Et, not to be intimidated by that man."

"I am sorry," she said. "He came here and waved a badge, showed some official papers. I didn't know he would upset you."

Wichai spoke very quietly. "It isn't her fault, Ajan Peter."

I could see from the woman's doleful eyes that she indeed regretted the breech in courtesy Mark Fisher's interview had caused. "Forgive me for speaking to you like that," I said. "That man made me very angry. He insulted Wichai."

When she heard that, her regret over the situation was plainly evident. Tears came to her eyes and I quickly assured her the fault was not hers.

The mood improved as we planned for the trip back home. We would pick the woman up at her home in the morning and catch the Rapid Train back upcountry.

"Won't you have some tea before you leave," she insisted. "It's such a nice British custom."

We did. And the talk turned to how the ministry was operated. I unconsciously now took advantage of every opportunity to learn more about Thailand and its workings. When Wichai was not my teacher, I asked questions from others. There was a time when I saw this as a tacit admission of ignorance which I couldn't tolerate. As I grew liberated from such constraints, I found my knowledge and my number of friends enlarged.

We arrived back in Roi-Et with Ajan Kularb after a pleasant trip with the urbane woman, and had some time to spare before the temple ceremony. We had become friends on the train ride up, and she extended an open invitation to visit her home whenever we were in Bangkok.

The Headmaster was delighted to see the woman, as an old acquaintance as well as the possible benefactor for his temple. Wichai and I could see them talk long into the evening on his veranda. It occurred to me that I had assumed the man more or less without passion, something the young always assume of the old. His wife had died over ten years before of malaria, and his saintly demeanor seemed to lift him above human appetites.

But, as in most things, my impressions were incorrect, or at least off base. Here was a man with an attractive and educated woman who was his peer. And Ajan Kularb was a widow.

"They look very happy together, don't they, Wichai," I said as we returned from a snack at the market.

"Yes, Ajan Peter. I think you see people as happy when you are happy. I think you are happy with Wichai, yes?"

"Wichai," I said, "You are the most wonderful, intelligent, and the handsomest boy in the world!"

He laughed, but I could see he ate up the praise. "I must be, Ajan Peter," he replied. "Because I don't think a man as intelligent and handsome as you would choose anyone else for a dying friend!"

It was my time to glow, and to laugh with him.

15

After a time of routine life at the college, Ajan Prasit informed staff and students that the day the provincial abbot deemed auspicious had arrived. I was proud to see so many of my fourth-year students playing an important part in the ceremony, setting up the temple grounds and tending the stands selling flowers, incense, and refreshments. Wichai helped with other young students as they cleared the grounds and set up a bamboo fence surrounding the temple building.

As Ajan Prasit moved about, making sure that everything was arranged properly, I noticed him glancing around with uncharacteristic anxiety. It was as though he were looking for someone not yet arrived.

I got him as he paused for a moment to sip some tea. "Is everything going all right?" I asked. "Is there anything I can do to help?"

"All is progressing according to plan, Ajan Peter," he smiled. "There is nothing you can do but enjoy. You already did your job bringing Ajan Kularb here."

I risked pressing him further. "You look worried, Head-master."

He took another sip of tea. "My friend from Songkla —Pra Anan—has not yet arrived. It is important to me that he be here for the dedication."

That's a long journey, I thought, all the way from the Southern Peninsula. Then it hit me—his lover! The one he

96

had told me about when he assured me that such a love is not unusual nor unhealthy.

"It is your friend who served as novice to you while you were a monk?" I asked.

"Yes," he nodded sadly. "He promised me he would come by the morning train, and it arrived some time ago."

The man's attention was drawn by the arrival of the governor and his company, so I was left to chat with the students and wait for things to begin.

The cho faa was on a small platform, ready to be inscribed with the meritorious name. Students and villagers were crowded around it, each affixing a small square of gold leaf to it till it began to glimmer and shine in the sun. I watched as Wichai applied his gold to the forehead of the gently arching creature.

At eight locations around the temple, and one in the very center of the ordination chapel, great round stones the size of watermelons were suspended over holes dug into the earth beneath them. These also became gilded as the devout pressed fluttering gold over them.

The auspicious moment was close. Ajan Prasit, dressed in white robes, was joined by the governor, a representative of the Royal Family, and the abbot in front of the temple. The King's representative read a long and weighty proclamation ceding the land to the use of the Lord Buddha.

This was a practice the Headmaster had told me went back to the days when the King was the sole and absolute owner of all land in the kingdom. Only when a temple was established did he relinquish his sovereignty over that portion of land and dedicate it to the service of worship.

After the proclamation, the party of elders paced from stone to stone within the compound, blessing each one, and purifying the perimeter against evil. I was mildly amused to learn that the fence was there to prevent women or animals from contaminating the holy ground.

Ajan Prasit concentrated on the affairs at hand, but I could imagine he was still anxious over the arrival of his old friend.

97

Wichai slipped to my side. "After they bless the final stone, they are all chopped loose and fall into the ground," he said. "Then all within their perimeter is the Lord Buddha's."

Long flashing blades raised, nine men awaited the signal. When it came, they hacked through the hemp rope and each stone dropped into the ground. Immediately there was chanting by the monks sitting off to one side, and cheers from the crowd.

"Will the bidding begin soon?" I asked the boy.

"As soon as we have something to eat," he said.

Thais seldom let much time pass without indulging in a bit to eat or drink. The practice seemed to be a natural social lubricant, as well as allowing any ritual to become nicely paced. Wichai and I ate some fruit and peanuts while we waited, and the monks were served their last meal of the day before fasting until the next morning. As the novices served them, I wondered again when the Headmaster's friend would show up.

The auction began. Excitement built in the crowd as the first tier of bidders fell out as the amounts raised into the thousands of baht. Ajan Kularb was demure and self-assured as the number of bidders was reduced to four, then three. She slowly slid a fan from her purse and spread it open.

And the two men she bid against continued to up the ante right along with her, until there were into the tens of thousands of baht. A hush fell over the audience and their eyes widened at the mention of such vast sums of money. Ajan Prasit had a gratified look on his face and his eyes fairly danced.

The flutter of banners or an occasional bark of a dog were the only sounds to break the silence. While we sat in the sun, the villagers hunkered in the shade of trees.

Sixty, seventy, then eighty-thousand. One of the men dropped out, leaving Ajan Kularb and one other. They began to hesitate in their bids, as though weighing the consequences of so much money against the enormous merit they would earn if they persevered. Ajan Kularb began to fan herself with determined little flicks of her wrist.

"Ninety thousand," said the man. He was a rich merchant in Roi-Et. He wanted someone from the province to have the honor of having his name inscribed on the cho faa. But he had his limits. It was so quiet after his bid, I could hear baby chicks peeping from across the compound.

When Ajan Kularb's voice followed his, the bid was made in a strong and victorious tone: "One hundred thousand baht," she proclaimed, and snapped her fan shut in a gesture of finality. Five thousand dollars! A significant amount, and more than enough to complete building the temple.

Fireworks exploded! Drums beat! A crew of students struggled with the rope attached to a pulley at the top of the temple to raise the cho faa skyward after Ajan Kularb had set her name in its base.

At that moment, a handsome priest walked between the crowds and approached the Headmaster. Ajan Prasit saw the man, and walked to meet him. He waied respectively, then grasped the monk's arm tightly. It was Pra Anan, arrived at last!

Smoke and noise were everywhere, and wildly garish colors streamed from standards set around the yard. Wichai and I stood with arms around each other as we watched Ajan Prasit embrace his old lover. Then, with a joyous cry, the cho faa was set into place, proudly capping the peak of the temple. Just as proudly, the Headmaster went around with the monk at his side, introducing him to all the dignitaries and staff. I waied deeply as I met him, and we shared a smile before he moved on.

The ritual complete, Ajan Prasit hosted a party at his home for the dignitaries and his friend. Wichai and I decided to celebrate ourselves with a bike ride into town for a restaurant meal. The rainy season was coming and clouds billowed high into threatening thunderclouds. But this had happened frequently lately, with no results.

"Order anything you like, Wichai," I said. I felt lavish on this day the temple saw the promise of completion. Perhaps too it was just a natural desire to please the boy—and myself. And perhaps it was seeing Ajan Prasit's happy reunion. Whatever the reason, I wanted to celebrate.

"I like seafood, Ajan Peter, and we rarely eat it here."

"What seafood? Shrimp, crab, fish?"

"I like crab best." Then the boy frowned.

"What's the matter, Wichai? Don't you think they'll have crab here?"

"Oh, I think they have it," he mumbled.

"Then order it."

"I cannot."

I thought there was some obscure religious reason. Wichai was seldom so serious about such things. "Tell me why?" I insisted.

"The man who waits on us, Ajan Peter, he is the owner."

"Yes?"

"You see his face," the boy said quietly.

I looked. The man's face was rather flattened. It looked like he'd suffered a broken nose and never had it tended to properly.

"The people in town call him Crabface," admitted the boy. "I cannot order crab from someone named Crabface."

I checked to see, and, yes, Wichai was very serious about this. At first dumbfounded, I was then amused. "Wichai," I laughed, "I'll order the crab for us, don't worry."

We both forgot about Crabface as we scooped up his succulent curried crab and shrimp with fluffy rice. But it gave me another example of the boy's gentle nature, another example for me to relate to my own behavior. Even in a harmless gesture which might be construed as a putdown.

"Remember, Ajan Peter," he reminded me, "the Eight-Fold Path. The Buddha says to speak the right words. A person must avoid remarks that seem funny but will hurt or insult another person."

The cafe was crowded with the arrival of groups of men as we ate. I recognized some as government officials and staff from the boy's school in town. I overheard them talking about a farang, then caught the name "Ben" in their conversation. I tried to catch what they were saying.

Wichai heard it too.

"What are they saying about Ben Ferrall, Wichai?"

The men became more eloquent as they had more Mekong whiskey, but their Laotian words were also more slurred.

"They say that a farang, that Ben, was in town. They say he was like a crazy man, wanting to sleep with women and drink whiskey. They say he spoke of running away or hiding from the army, that he didn't want to fight anymore."

"Anything else?" I asked. "Did he go back to Bantawat?"

"They say he mentioned going to find a farang friend," said Wichai. "He had another man with him, a Thai man, like a bandit, also drunk."

I felt a chill, then a rush of anger. Was that man going to implicate me in his demented escapade? What was he up to?

"Forget him, Wichai," I said, pushing the idea of everything but this evening out of my mind. "Let's order ice cream for dessert!"

We did, and I had coffee laced with condensed milk. Except for the fleeting invasion of Ben Ferrall, it was one of the finest meals I've ever experienced.

Lightning had cut the sky as we ate, but again, it did this often without a drop of rain falling. As we left the restaurant and I unlocked the bicycle, though, I felt a fat, warm drop splash the nape of my neck.

"What?" I asked, jerking up. I thought Wichai was playing a trick.

The boy looked at me innocently. "I think the rainy season is beginning, Ajan Peter," he said.

It was! With a rumbling crash of thunder, the skies opened. Sheets of rain washed down over us as we struggled back home in the dark. The dusty laterite road was turned to muck. It stuck to itself on the tires and soon was so thick it jammed up under the fenders.

Forced to walk through the mud, Wichai began humming a Thai folk song. I trudged on silently, trained as I was to view walking in the rain as an unpleasant experience.

By the time we were home, however, I'd released yet another constraint, and was chatting and singing along with the boy. How clean the rain was, I thought, and how exhilarating! We soaped up each other in the shower and spent the rest of the evening in our pakamas, talking and reading.

As I turned off the light before getting into bed beside Wichai, I glanced over at Ajan Prasit's house. There he was under the bare light of his veranda, after his long-awaited day, alone now with Pra Anan, talking long into the rain-washed evening.

16

The next day the staff and student body waited for Ajan Prasit's routine morning announcements. He was usually prompt, so we passed the time in nervous chatting. Thai patience is beyond mine, and I forced myself to talk with other teachers about our work. I respected the diligence of those in the English Department especially, and had learned to pace my teaching from their examples. I ended up, in spite of my impatience, by getting some useful hints from Ajan Piboon about how to handle our first-year classes.

"They need so much drill, Ajan Peter," he said. "The English language is so foreign to their tongues, they need to practice its sounds over and over."

"Yes, I'm learning that," I confessed. I always wanted to move the more eager students along to conversation. But that was a giant leap from the simple drill that many of them were used to.

"Keep the fourth-year students active with reading and conversation," the man advised, "and they will be an example for the younger ones."

"And those in my evening classes, too," I said. This voluntary program was my most successful venture. With the pressures of academic progress relieved, I found both myself and my students thrived in an atmosphere of relaxed learning after chores.

As we talked, a hush fell over the campus. I followed the others in looking down the dusty road which lead to Ajan

Prasit's home. We all saw the approach of a monk, walking alone, walking slowly. It was Pra Anan.

When the robed man reached the assistant headmaster, the two spoke quietly together for a moment. Then the assistant nodded and walked to the podium to address the assembly.

He stood there and swallowed several times, then began speaking. "Pra Anan has told me that Ajan Prasit is very ill this morning. Perhaps the stress of the temple ceremony weakened his condition. We know how he had been devoted to both the school and to his Buddhist brothers. Pra Anan asks that we do not worry about Ajan Prasit, but continue in our jobs, to strive for excellence."

He paused, blinking rapidly, then turned to the president of the student body. "Nariwan will continue with today's announcements."

A sad murmur flowed like a wave among us. An earlier illness, I learned, had put Ajan Prasit in bed for several weeks the year before. There was fear for his life then. With this relapse, his condition was more critical than ever.

The pale of the Headmaster's illness lay over the college like a cloud for the next few days. Wichai was subdued and went about his duties without comment. We didn't have the heart to make love, and I didn't miss it. There was an unspoken understanding that we could serve Ajan Prasit best by applying ourselves to our work.

My classes progressed with a seriousness I hadn't encountered before. I began to wonder if it was me. The gentle teasing I used to indulge in was gone. I rewarded superior performances with a mere nod of my head. My conversations with Wichai were mechanical, and I knew this couldn't go on for long.

I decided to inquire if I could talk with Ajan Prasit, if he was well enough to receive visitors. Pra Anan assured me that the Headmaster would see me the next day.

That night Wichai and I ended up holding each other, kissing and fondling without urgency. I felt an unaccustomed awkwardness with the boy, yet loved him more than ever.

It was as if we, along with the whole college, were an extension of the Headmaster himself, and the entire organism slowed and stuttered with his sickness.

"You are not unhappy with me, Ajan Peter?" asked the boy.

"No, Wichai. I'm concerned about Ajan Prasit, that's all. I love you, Wichai, more than anything in the world."

"The Headmaster is a good man," said the boy. "I think he has taught many people in his life how to live like a good Buddhist. I think he will continue to teach many even long after his death."

"You think he will die?" I asked.

"The news is not good, Ajan Peter. He is old, and has worked hard. He could have retired like most officials years ago, but he chose to keep working." The boy thought, his brow pulling down over his beautiful face. "Maybe he would die sooner if he did not have his work here at the college and at the temple."

I sighed, hoping to ease the ache within me. "Perhaps you are right."

Wichai turned to me and we looked into each others eyes. He had never been more lovely, sadness and concern gleaming in his large, dark eyes. I leaned forward and brushed my lips across his eyebrows, then over his creased forehead. His muscles smoothed under my caress. Lifting his face, he met my lips with his and we kissed long and lovingly, without lust or greed.

We didn't make love. Not in the way the phrase is usually, if euphemistically, used. We held each other, glad for each other's warmth, but there was no climax. Instead, it was as if by merely touching we drained some of the hurt from each other and put something living and vital in its place. I never felt love as such a powerful creative force before, and have seldom since.

Wichai fell asleep in my arms when we'd held each other for more than an hour. I eased out from his bed and looked down through the shadows at his body sprawled carelessly over the sheets. He seemed to burn and pulse with life, while so vulnerable and naked. His arms and legs, how thin they were. His slender fingers fluttered as he dreamed. As he turned, I could see his heartbeat through his ribs. How could such a small thing as this boy command my soul? So many paradoxes, I thought, like that of life and death itself. I drew the sheet up over him and went to my own bed.

Next morning was Saturday. Since I had no classes, I was free to approach the Headmaster's house first thing in the morning. The campus had an eerie silence about it. There was no sign of any activity at the house, so I hesitated. Then I saw Pra Anan's shaved head above the railing of the veranda. Removing my shoes and climbing the stairs, I saw him meditating, alone. A low humming seemed to breath from somewhere around us.

I immediately dropped to sit cross-legged across from the priest. It is a grave insult to intentionally rise above the level of another's head, especially that of a monk. I waited in silence, listening to the hollow moaning absorb deep silence into its void. Something strange and unwilled was occurring inside me. There was a tug at my soul — a musical note sent spinning about my head — and I let go, allowing it to happen.

Time diminished to a point, then stretched out to an imperceptible distance. Hypnotically, I fell into the abyss, enfolded, it seemed by a joyous freedom beyond sensation. There was no resistance to the alluring sense of release in this journey, and no desires any longer burned through my spleen. I dwelled for a time — how long? — in that blissful state, suspended from the world, knowing — or sensing — the impact of a true and sweeter reality. It was as though a gift had been made at this time and place — the gift of meditation, for I had certainly put no effort into attaining such a state.

As it had come, the dream-like state diffused. I again clearly saw leaves lifting on the branches of the tamarind tree beside the house, and heard the cocks crowing. Gravity still solidly holding everything in its place, Pra Anan was there before me.

He lifted his head and his eyes slitted open. "Ajan Prasit has died," he said calmly.

The words were like a massive weight penetrating the elastic sphere of my consciousness, distorting and ripping it to shreds. Yet something remained to cushion their blows, some inner peace I had only heard of before, something which made the Headmaster's death fit into a larger, natural plan, the comprehension of which was not important.

I nodded, and felt the soft impact of tears hit the backs of my folded hands.

"Ajan Peter," Pra Anan said, "we do not worship the Buddha, you know, for he was a man. A great man, certainly — a sage — but a man, like you and me . . . and Ajan Prasit. We venerate him. We seek guidance from his example and his words of wisdom."

"Yes," I answered.

"So we should also venerate the example Ajan Prasit gave us of his life. I am happy that he is released from this life to rise further toward nirvana, and happy that I knew and learned from such a great friend and teacher."

"I am happy too, Pra Anan, for what I learned from him," I answered. "And sad."

"That is natural, Ajan Peter. I feel an unspeakable loss, and must fill it with memories and merit of my own making. Come, have something to eat with me. We will celebrate our friend's death the next few days in public view. Let us take a moment now to talk alone together."

We talked, of course, about Ajan Prasit. But as the initial sting of grief was eased by this gentle monk, the talk turned to me and my life. I shared without reserve, and met his intelligent curiosity with an honesty I rarely felt with strangers. But we were not strangers, really. Our lives intertwined with Ajan Prasit, and through the spiritual experience I dwelt in for a few minutes out there on the veranda.

17

When I shared the news with Wichai, he cried also.

"Ajan Prasit was a great man, Ajan Peter. I will miss him very much," he said, holding me.

But after his tears, a stoicism came over him which I first mistook for lack of sensitivity. Ignoring it, only later did I realize that the boy, like all village youth, had an intimate knowledge of death, and, with his Buddhist belief in reincarnation, dealt with it more pragmatically than the Western mind. Here there was no mystic heaven, no vain euphemistic hereafter to lift the experience of death into drama. Death is merely one stage in a journey eons long. Even in the midst of my spontaneous meditation I could sense that compelling reality, and feel the power of its logic.

The funeral rites were elaborate nonetheless. At Roi Et's central temple, Ajan Prasit's ceremonial casket was the center of activity for several days. Worshippers by the hundreds came to pay respects, laying offerings of incense and flowers at its base.

Monks chanted sutras and officials, both civil and priestly, prepared for his cremation. The emissaries of the King who had presided over Ajan Prasit's temple ceremony remained for his funeral. Colleagues and friends from all over Thailand swelled the population of the city, giving it a festive air.

And indeed there was little of the somber lamentation common to funerals I'd attended back home. As the night of the cremation arrived, films were shown on a sheet stretched across one of the gates of the temple, and vendors were busy selling sweets and drinks.

Wichai and I were there, as he had been all day. I was dressed, as were all the dignitaries and college staff, in my suit and tie. Custom dictated that my place was with the members of the faculty, too; but I knew they would understand if I often remained close to Wichai, whose union with me had been blessed by the Headmaster himself.

"In America there is sadness at funerals," I said as I turned to Wichai.

"We are sad, too, that we have lost a friend and teacher," he said with a smile. "But aren't you happy that he is further on his journey?"

And Pra Anan was there also, as he had been throughout the period of mourning, effectively guiding the events which would culminate in the release of his closest friend's soul by fire.

He rose now, as the sun lay setting, and approached the microphone beside the elaborate coffin. A hush settled over the crowd as he waited to speak. When he spoke, his voice was gently penetrating: "Friends and colleagues of Ajan Prasit Siriwat, and especially his family. I knew Prasit from the time he entered the monastery, and have enjoyed his friendship all the years since. Never have I met a man who better exemplified the Middle Path. No words I can say will pay proper tribute to his time among us, and I think he would approve if I read the words of the Lord Buddha at His imminent death:

> My disciples, my end is approaching, our parting is near, but do not lament. Life is ever changing, none can escape the dissolution of the body. This I am now to manifest by my own death, my body falling apart like a decaying cart.
>
> Do not vainly lament, but do wonder at the rule of transiency and learn from it the emptiness of human life. Do not cherish the unworthy desire that the changeable might become unchanging.

The evil of worldly desires is always seeking chances to deceive the mind. If a viper lives in your room and you wish to have a peaceful sleep, you must first chase it out.

You must break the bonds of worldly passions and drive them away as you would a viper. You must positively protect your own mind.

My disciples, my last moment has come, but do not forget that death is only the vanishing of the physical body. The body was born from parents and was nourished by food; just as inevitable are sickness and death.

But the true Buddha is not a human body — it is Enlightenment itself. A human body must vanish, but the Wisdom of Enlightenment will exist forever in the truth of the Dharma, and in the practice of the Dharma. He who see merely my body does not truly see me. Only he who accepts my teaching truly sees me.

After my death, the Dharma shall be your teacher. Follow the Dharma and you will be true to me.

During the last forty-five years of my life, I have withheld nothing from my teaching. There is no secret teaching, no hidden meaning; everything has been taught openly and clearly. My dear disciples, this is the end. In a moment, I shall be passing into Nirvana. This is my instruction.

Pra Anan stood like a statue when he finished, then slowly sat as a surge of chanting rose from within the temple.

After sunset, and in the privacy of the coconut grove behind the ordination chapel, we awaited the auspicious moment of cremation.

Wichai and I sat, our knees touching, as we watched the final preparations. The crematory casket was a simple box, now removed from the ceremonial coffin, and was placed upon the pyre of stacked wood. In the light of a single lamp, we saw the lid lifted. Pra Anan purified the corpse with coconut milk, then placed coins over both Ajan Prasit's closed eyes. The lid was closed and the pyre splashed with kerosene.

Pra Anan stepped back, dropped to his knees and waied deeply. This was unusual, for monks bow to no man, only to the Lord Buddha himself. We joined the priest in our last respects to the Headmaster's vital spirit.

The abbot lit a candle and handed it to the priest. He held it before him as he approached us. He appeared ghostly and smoothly emotionless as he stood above us with its warm glow bathing his open face. He held the candle out to me.

I hesitated, unsure of what to do.

"Take it, Ajan Peter," he said, "and light the fire. It is Ajan Prasit who asks it of you. He wished you, who had traveled half the world to renew memories within him, to carry the flame of his final journey."

I grasped it and rose. I motioned Wichai to join me. Together, we walked close enough to the coffin for the fumes of the fuel to lift on the evening air before us. I took the boy's hand and wrapped his fingers around my wrist, then lowered the flame to the base of the pyre.

The fire licked into the fuel-soaked wood and snaked up and around to soon enfold the entire stack. It drew air and bit into the fibers of the wood. A crackle and roar sucked up through the pile and caressed the coffin itself with curtains of flame.

There were tears flowing, unrestrained, for the unresolvable paradox of happiness and sadness consuming us. The fronds above danced in the billowing heat of the fire. The light of the fire shimmered on the palm's shiny undersides. The pyre was now consumed in a swirling ball of flame, and embers began to gnaw at the very cortex of wood and bone.

Wichai and I held hands as Ajan Prasit was freed from his earthly bonds, his spirit purified by fire. As much as the man had taught me, I thought, there was much I had yet to realize of his teaching.

18

The college was closed for a period of mourning, and it was hard for many of us to overcome the torpor at the loss of Ajan Prasit. I didn't envy the assistant Headmaster's job; he would have to fill shoes made mythically large by his predecessor's wisdom.

I was restless — that old feeling I was going nowhere, and some of the old anxieties began to creep into my circular thoughts. Was I wasting my time here, after all? Was my relationship with Wichai at a dead end? Was I merely suffocating the kid with my possessive lust or stunting the boy's emotional growth? And when would the war in Vietnam begin to haunt me again, in the forms of Fisher and Ferrall?

While returning to America was always certain, I thought it best to leave before anyone was hurt, or perhaps worse, bored. Then an hour later I would decide that, no, sitting around graduate school was not the answer either. A chill ran through me when I remembered the attitude toward gays in my home country. I hadn't even dared tell my family.

I received three letters the week I wrestled with this problem. The first was from my father:

Dear Son,

Hope you are doing well. Your mother has a little cold but I'm fine. Been working on my golf game some with the nicer weather. Heather [my sister] sends her love, as well as Grover [my dog].

I've always backed your decision to go to Thailand, Peter, and I still think it was the right thing to do. Heaven knows, if the same opportunity presented itself to me when I was your age, I would have jumped at it. But something has happened to concern me.

Maybe it's nothing, but it's got me to thinking you're into things that might jeopardize your future, and I want you to think clearly about whatever it is you're doing.

The FBI is doing a background check on you. Some of the neighbors have been interviewed. They even went to Frank Ellington, even though you just worked for him summers through college. They're asking about your politics, any organizations you belong to, that sort of thing. They're even snooping into your sex life! Can you believe it?

Now maybe it's nothing, like I said, just you being so near the war zone and all, but I can't imagine the government going to this sort of trouble for any American college kid teaching English. You don't have to tell me what it is, if there is something. Mother doesn't know about the FBI and she doesn't know I'm writing this letter.

Just remember, son — you have our full support. If the government is looking for something unusual, they won't find it in your background anyway. We've always been proud of you, Peter.

Write again soon. Just give some thought to the consequences this inquiry might have.

Love,
Dad

That was father's tone, all right — concerned love. The FBI investigation had Mark Fisher's smell to it, and I couldn't imagine any other reason. I was scared and angry.

Then I read the second letter, from Dr. Atkinson, my English advisor at college:

Dear Peter,
I haven't written since your arrival there, I know; the work has been a bit more arduous since the enrollment is augmented so suddenly by enlightened young men seeking knowledge rather than experience in the fields of Vietnam. If

113

idealism doesn't get them into the hallowed halls of learning, I suppose that fear will do.

I hope your experiences there are positive ones. In spite of its age, the old saying is correct: experience *is* the best teacher. The precepts of Buddhism you acquire through even casual contact can be an invaluable tool in daily living. I know I'll never regret the years I spent in Europe as a young student. The poverty of those years is forgotten, weighed against the self-knowledge I gained.

Something more practical and political, Peter: there is a man, an FBI man, on campus. He'd shown his credentials, so it's not the usual undercover thing looking into student subversives and such. He's been asking questions about you, your politics, organizations, that sort of thing. Naturally, I refused to discuss anything with the man beyond your academic achievement, but he asked about your personal life. Can you imagine? My own ignorance of it left me guiltless in admitting it.

I only write to tell you this that it may forewarn you. Perhaps it is entirely proper, and merely clearance pursuant to a diplomatic career. I thought it wise to share my apprehensions with you, one of the students I've felt showed most promise in my years of teaching.

Continue with your work in the best spirit of learning, Peter. Let me know of your progress from time to time.

Best regards,
Dean

It was almost eerie, how the same tone rang from both letters. I felt almost hunted, the feeling made worse because I felt I'd done no wrong. Was that right?

The third letter was on Army stationary, unsigned, but had to be from Fisher, or through him. It was, in fact, no letter at all, but a copy of a document—it looked like a cover letter to a report—with a note attached:

Re: Lt. Benjamin Carey Ferrall
Serial #29/8194-D4
Profile Subject to: 36B

Lt. Ferrall enlisted in the Army in his home town of Stockton, California in March, 1964. He showed an eagerness to follow orders and an aptitude for individual initiative. The only incidences of disobedience in training were three AWOL charges, later dropped, when Lt. Ferrall initiated others to remain outside the base beyond the prescribed periods of leave.

Lt. Ferrall was assigned duty in Vietnam after training. His abilities to adapt to the climate and guerilla warfare made him an outstanding soldier. He earned the Purple Heart at Da Nang, and was awarded several medals for bravery on other occasions (see APPENDIX B).

The subject was promoted to Lieutenant upon his assignment for special training (see APPENDIX F).

It was after Lt. Ferrall had accomplished his fourth mission in Special Services that he came to the attention of the psychiatric panel. He was displaying signs of fatigue and disobedience beyond the norm for his position and earlier profile.

Tests indicated Lt. Ferrall was paranoid, with a pre-clinical indication for manic-depressive syndrome. It was determined that the subject was not presently a danger to his mission, but required monitoring. Earlier indications of disobedience could magnify into dangerously elusive activity.

Lt. Ferrall was reported AWOL following a reported depressive incident (see APPENDIX G). In leaving his unit, the subject seriously wounded a comrade seeking to restrain him.

The following recommendations are made:

1. Lt. Ferrall be considered dangerous.

2. Upon apprehension, he should be thoroughly debriefed by this unit only.

3. A Court Martial must be weighed against the information known to the subject which would become the record of these proceedings.

The note, handwritten, was at the bottom:

This doesn't say you know anything more than you say you know. It is information, clear and simple.

This was Fisher's way of telling me the man was dangerous, I suppose. And that he'd reached back to my friends and family to cover his bets, if he found I did know about Ben. Well, he was unlikely to find anything to use as a wedge against me there; I'd been a closet-case all along, if homosexuality was going to be an issue. And my political views were about as wild as Jack Kennedy's had been.

But it galled me, this whole affair. I didn't want to see my father and friends dragged into this. It already had tainted my relationship with Wichai. This, on top of Ajan Prasit's death, made these days the lowest of my stay in Thailand, and I looked back on my earlier bout of self-pity with longing.

It was while I was brooding over all this that Wichai came up with an idea. We had gone to the market and were having a dish of noodles for lunch after both of us had been to the barber. His hair was clipped short in regulation student style.

"Let's go to my home, Ajan Peter. Rice planting is near, and it is the time for Songkran Festival," he said brightly.

"What is Songkran? I asked. There's always some celebration or other, I thought. Perhaps it is in these festivals that the society is more unified, maybe childlike, but it seemed to help bind people together and allow a release of energy.

"Songkran is much fun. It is a water festival, to celebrate the start of the planting season," he said, smiling.

I detected some of the familiar mischief in him as he described how people were glad of the rains after the long dry season, especially here in the Northeast. The region was largely unaffected by the southwest monsoons, which nourished the South and Central regions of Thailand, because of the Korat Plateau. Also, there was no major river system to leave its silt after flooding. It was only those monsoon winds from the northeast which penetrated into 'the ear of the elephant,' as it is called, to allow a single planting a year. The farmers' lives depended on it.

"There is even a bonfai festival here in the Northeast, Ajan Peter," explained Wichai. He loved to teach me about his people. "Large rockets are made and sent into the sky to ask the gods to send more rain. The highest rocket wins the contest."

"Let's go," I said. "And remind me to get some flowers from the market for your mother."

19

A visit to Bantawat sounded like a perfect solution to my mood of grieving anxiety. As we headed down the river, I thought of Ben Ferrall but didn't say anything to the boy. There was something illogically superstitious in not talking about him, as though that would prevent his appearance when we arrived at the otherwise peaceful little village.

And indeed, he did not appear during our first couple days, effortlessly spent in blending into Wichai's family life and helping plant and transplant the rice.

Village life seemed rather ordinary to me by now. Seeing the women dress in no more than a pasin tied about their waists was no longer quaint. I couldn't help thinking of old *National Geographic*s on my first visits to the villages.

But Wichai would often devise a new twist to days which followed one another like stepping in and out of a dream.

We were just back from the fields when he pointed up. "Do you want a coconut, Ajan Peter?" he asked.

"Will you get me one?" I challenged.

He immediately gathered his pakama between his legs and tucked it in back. "You watch. Wichai will become a monkey!"

He approached the tree, embraced it, then planted his feet flat against it, knees out, looking more like a tree frog than a monkey.

"Be careful," I said. I sounded like a father.

The boy shimmied up the trunk in a way I knew he must have done often as a child. And the trees here grew straight up, not in the graceful and easier arc as the wind-whipped trees of the coast.

"Watch, Ajan Peter," the boy yelled. Supporting himself just under the umbrella-like fronds, he began to twist off one of the large nuts.

It fell with a thud at my feet. I applauded him and he grinned down at me. Then he chattered like a monkey.

"We have all we need here, Ajan Peter," he said from his perch. "Look, my father gave me a wonderful tool." He held out his hand, fingers spread. "It is a comb, a spoon, a sunshade, and a thousand other things."

He pointed to his forehead. "And here, Ajan Peter, is the most wonderful thing of all."

"And what's in there, Wichai?" I yelled up at him.

"The universe," he said.

When he'd pried off two more nuts, we took them to his home before going back to work in the fields. It was back-breaking work, stooping over for hours, sloshing through the sucking mud in the heat, and shoving bunches of young rice plants deep into the ooze.

"Curl your toes to help keep your balance," Wichai told me. He was happy helping his family and neighbors, and never complained that the work was too hard or the sun too hot. I would take frequent breaks and watch him. The boy's body was part of this place: his tanned skin against the vibrant green of the rice shoots, his slender grace below the bending palms, his adolescent beauty in the lush promise of full and fertile growth. I determined, watching him work, that I would take time to rediscover every inch of him, with my hands and my lips, when we were under the mosquito nets that night.

Back to work, I allowed my body to discover a rhythm in the planting. Left to themselves, my muscles moved in an economical and enjoyable cycle that had me planting more shoots with less work in a straight line alongside the boy. It was as though our bodies were communicating, as they did

119

when we made love, without a word spoken. I thought again of Ajan Prasit, of his passage through life. Perhaps letting go was as much a part of the secret as was striving. "I step into the river and I step out," he once said, "and the river flows on."

"Well, good to see you, Pete!" came a voice from the dike.

I lifted upright and spun around. It was Ben Ferrall, grinning through his whiskers, hunkering like an ape looking down on us.

"So you are still here," was all I could say.

"Oh, yeah. Still here . . . and there," he said vaguely. He sucked deeply on a joint, then held the smoke deeply before blowing it out. "Getting to feel a little cramped, though, Pete. Don't know if I can hide out here much longer. Feel as though they're coming at me, coming to get me and take me back to Nam."

The man was not well, I thought. He was very thin, his skin the color of watered, raw silk. And his clothes were a combination of his ragged combat gear and village dress. He didn't look like he bathed regularly.

A man appeared from the bushes and approached Ferrall, then hunkered down beside him. He had a large knife in his belt.

"This here's Tawit," Ben explained. "He's my Thai buddy. Says he wants to fight like me, be a soldier and kill like his here Ben." He laughed as he said this. It was a dry, hollow laugh.

Tawit merely nodded and glared at me and Wichai. His eyes were flat and cold. Ben handed him the joint and he drew the fumes into his lungs.

"Hello, Tawit," said Wichai. "How is your family?"

Apparently the man was from the village. Wichai's question sent a softness into Tawit's eyes, let him drop his guard. He passed the butt back to Ben and said, "They are good, Wichai. And yours?"

While the Thais talked, I climbed up the bank to talk to Ben. When I got near, I could tell he was dirty. He smelled of old sweat and stale beer, and the sweet hemp of marijuana. I winced, but sat beside him.

"So tell me, Pete," he said, "you run into anyone who's after my balls, anyone like the army or the CID or anything?"

"There is a man, a man named Mark Fisher, who's talked to me," I told him. "He's from the CID, apparently. I haven't said anything about you, though. What will happen if they catch you?"

"They'll kill me, like I said!" he snapped. Then, calmer —"Court martial. Prison, maybe. Me and Tawit, we're gonna head north. Told him he could fight like a guerrilla up there in Laos, be a real kung fu soldier like he's seen in the movies."

"And you? I thought you were sick of killing?"

"Hell, yes," he blurted out. "I figure I can hide out in a little village up there, away from here. Figure I could become like a head man of a village, have respect, all the women I want. I don't ever want to go back." His laugh was thin as paper.

There was the patina of madness on Ben Ferrall. I could see that. When I saw him before, I figured his ravings were due to panic. Now, after all these months, his paranoia had settled into a neurotic pattern of thought that had him indulging in dangerous delusions.

"Why don't you just turn yourself in, Ben?" I said. "Say you had amnesia or something, and you want to get well again."

"That again? Fuck that!" he spat. The violence of his reaction startled me. "No way I'm going back to those stinking bastards. They're out to hang me, Pete! No end to the killing they do."

After a moment of silence, I said, "You're sick, Ben. I think you ought to get to a hospital or something, and—"

"Fuck you!" he screamed. "Not you, not anyone going to mess around with my head anymore, you hear?"

I saw that Tawit's hand had gone to the handle of his knife. Wichai looked at me, fear in his eyes over what might happen with these men. A sick feeling churned through my stomach.

"Right, Ben," I said quietly. "I just wanted to help."

"It's the war, Pete, the fuckin' war," he rambled as he quieted. "It made everyone crazy—everyone."

I just nodded.

Field birds chirped in the pause. When Ben spoke again, it was quiet. "I used to think it was cars, and fancy dames, money in my pocket that I'd miss. It ain't those things, Pete. It's applesauce."

He looked at me as if he hoped I'd understand.

"Applesauce. The gathering of the apples with my daddy in our orchards, mashing them, the smell of it, and ma cooking them up into sauce."

I did understand. And that understanding, the strength of it frightened me.

There wasn't much use in talking anymore just then. "Let's finish this paddy," I said to Wichai as I stood. "I hope you find what you want, Ben," I said to the man as I left him with Tawit on the dike. I wanted more than ever to be rid of this intrusion into our lives here.

"Oh, I think we will, Pete. I think we will." he said to my back. His words carried a sinister determination, and I hoped the 'we' he used referred to him and Tawit.

When I looked up from the mud after several minutes of work, both men were gone.

That night I ate slowly, almost dazed by exhaustion.

"You don't have farmer's bones," said Wichai. "You will be stiff tomorrow."

"If I live till tomorrow," I said, stretching my sore legs out before me.

"Oh, you will," said the boy. "Besides, tomorrow is Songkran! It is a happy festival, Ajan Peter. We will not work on the holiday."

"Good," I replied. And instead of passionately exploring the boy's sinuous beauty that night, I huddled up to him and promptly fell asleep.

Something woke us in the middle of the night. I lay there and heard Wichai's breathing, knowing he was also awake.

"What was that sound?" I asked.

"I don't know, Ajan Peter," he whispered. "Perhaps an animal, or a branch against the roof."

It was silent. The nocturnal insects had long since settled down from their evening feeding. I reached out to stroke Wichai's bare arm and he turned to me with that deep hum that meant pleasure.

"Hold me, Ajan Peter," he said with an urgency unusual for him. It was I who usually initiated our lovemaking, though he would often tempt me to it. Now he molded himself into my arms, my lips brushing down his slender neck and over his skinny shoulder. I moved up to nibble his earlobe and he hugged me tighter.

"I will miss Ajan Prasit very much, Ajan Peter," he said softly. "I cannot think that he is dead."

"Me too, Wichai," I said. "His wisdom allowed me to love you."

"I love you, Peter." It was the first time he had called me by my given name alone. We were lovers—not teacher and student, native and foreigner, boy and man—we were equals bound by our mutual love, and our grief.

"I will always love you," I said. I remembered the day Ajan Prasit had talked about the life-long responsibilities of love. The thought of it was now a comfort rather than a burden.

We held each other, softly caressing, the heat of lust replaced by something more binding and more permanent. Holding Wichai like that, I felt surrounded by a deep benevolence, a feeling like the one I experienced the day of Ajan Prasit's death.

We were jarred awake again, before dawn. Enough murky gray dispelled the dark for us to see the glint of steel on the long knife held over us.

"Come," said the stern voice of Tawit.

I could see it was Ben's Thai buddy from his silhouette. The tone of his voice and the blade approaching my throat convinced me to do as he said. Wichai and I stood, pulling our pants on in the damp sweat of sleep and fear, while he stood patiently, but poised to prod us on with his crude weapon if we hesitated or resisted.

When we were dressed, he stood aside and followed us down the ladder and along the jungle path. We pushed the overgrowth aside as we went. Wichai went ahead of me, and seemed to know the way. No doubt he had traveled this way since he was a child. I followed his graceful form as a rosy pink began to flood over the eastern sky.

"Left," ordered Tawit. Wichai plunged us into a less-used path. After a hundred feet or so, we saw a rough hut only a couple feet off the ground. No wonder Fisher had never found it, if he'd been here. It was concealed from all sides, outside the village as though quarantined. Candles burned inside, their wavering light leaked through the many cracks and tears on the straw matting of the shanty.

We hesitated as we stood before it. Then I felt the point of the blade between my shoulders.

"Inside!"

We parted the cloth covering the door and entered.

Everything about my stay in Thailand was about to be changed.

20

"The war, Pete, it's changed everything," Ben said quietly after we entered.

We sat on the ragged straw matting facing him. The glowing candles he'd placed all around him gave off an eerie glow when mixed with the colors of the rising sun outside. It was as if the man was trying to guard himself against darkness. Tawit stood behind us, his blade lowered. There was a sick, waxy smell oozing from decaying matter around us.

Ben reached into a pack of cigarettes, withdrew the last one, and crumpled the empty package in his angry fist. His hollow eyes were down as he continued to speak. "I was a right good fellow before things got bad. I was gung-ho, even. Went into fighting with a vengeance. Liked the army life, too. Then something happened, Pete. Figured, hell, what's an angle-shooter like me doing messed up in this no-win, fucking war anyway?"

There was a drippy silence. Early morning was ready to flower into dawn. We waited, then the man raised his head and looked into my eyes. "The killing, Pete. Just fuckin' rotten killing. For no goddam reason. Too much. . . ."

"What do you want from us, Ben," I asked with a quaver in my voice.

It was as though he didn't hear me. "We was ordered into this village, see. Flush out the Cong, that's what they told us. Enemy agents thick as flies around a dead dog, they said. They hide out in tunnels spread all over the village,

125

then come up and mix with the farmers, no one knows the difference."

Was this My Lai he was talking about, I wondered? The details were just coming out in the papers of that horrible incident. Perhaps, I thought, there were many My Lais. . . .

"Flush out the Cong. Sanitize the area. With extreme prejudice." He chopped his words with a grinning bitterness that made his face look like a skull. "Well, we did. I was a good little soldier boy, Pete. My M-16 was hot in my hands and my boots were red up to my ankles in bloody mud. My buddy next to me fielded a flame-thrower, and it did the job on the huts as I cut down the folks that run out of 'em."

He sucked the cigarette deeply, then exhaled a long cloud of smoke in our faces. "Seems to me I recall wanting to be the best damn sanitizer in Nam. That's what I thought as I was slamming lead into those, those . . . people. We was about finished, the village flat and smoking all around us. There was the sound of Huey blades chopping up the air. Things flying around. Then I spotted this shack in back, kinda looked like an outhouse or something."

The cigarette burned low between his fingers.

"My buddies, they were withdrawing already, kinda like they was guilty or something, you know? Like dogs with their tails between their legs. I could see their shoulders slumped as they plodded off toward the field where the Hueys were gonna pick us up. They weren't like the ones I used to fight with. Not the kind of men my daddy fought with either, and we won that war, the Big One, you know.

"I wasn't gonna stop. I had information, Pete, still do, up here," he tapped his head, "that these gooks had a network of spies, how they operated, who their contacts were. I wasn't gonna let one of them bastards leave alive. Not if that meant they were gonna go off after some Yank when we left.

"So I circle around, heading for this shack. I don't hear anything, but hell, there's so much noise from shells and fire all around, it don't make no difference. This target was mine.

"I level my piece and rake the place. Really crisscross

it, man! Really hit it high and low! Gave it a punch of lead that had it tipping over!"

Ben seemed almost delirious reliving the experience. The cigarette burned his fingers before he looked down surprised, then flicked it away.

"The damn thing fell. There they were, Pete. Children. Fuckin' children, all huddled together, their faces buried in each other, all hugging a woman, a young woman, hardly more than a child herself. They were all dead," he said. His voice was flat now.

Wichai bowed his head. He seemed to be praying as we waited for Ben to continue. When he did, his voice trembled.

"She was pregnant, Pete. I—I'd split her open, ripped her belly. Her baby was oozing out, all bloody and wet, right down her lap, between the bodies of the clinging children. The face of the baby, Pete. It was right on me. The face. . . ."

He looked up, every sinew tight. He spoke in a whisper that was drawn snapping tight. "It was *my* face, Pete! That goddam unborn little baby—it had *my face* on it!"

It took me a moment to register what he'd described. When I did, a swarm of grotesqueries spun in my head. It was repulsive, yet fascinating, this image. Was he saying he had fathered that child? Or was there some ironic twist that made him see his own face in that of the most innocent of war's victims? Whatever it was, the specter of that murdered fetus haunted him, drove him to madness. That and the drugs he was taking, I figured. And maybe a hundred other things I'd never know.

War has many daily horrors, I realized. But this seemed to wrench the order of things with such violence, it made me shiver. I had to swallow air in rapid gulps to keep from vomiting.

After absorbing Ben's tale, I looked up to see that he was quieter, but a steely madness clouded his eyes.

"So, Pete, you got to help us, huh? Get us north? The CID, that Fisher fellow, he wouldn't dare interfere if there was civilians like you and the kid along with me."

Wichai looked to me, wondering how I would react. I gave him a quick shake of my head. "I don't want to get involved, Ben," I said to the man. "I'm sorry. I don't like Fisher and don't always agree with what he stands for, either. But I can't risk it; I have responsibilities to the college. And I don't want you putting Wichai in any danger."

Ferrall sat there dumbly. He appeared resigned to risk open escape alone after what I said. Then he raised his eyes and gave Tawit behind me a jerk of his head.

I felt the blade of Tawit's knife dig into my back.

"I think you will come with us, Pete, old boy," Ben said with a sick grin. "Otherwise I don't think you or your little buddy here are going to go anywhere."

"I think we should do as he says, Ajan Peter," said Wichai. "I have seen men like this, men who will do anything to get what they want. We will go with them, then be free again."

"Okay, Ben," I sighed. "Just don't get excited, huh? I won't try to be a hero."

We were now his hostages.

21

All the way to the riverbank I thought of the peace and serenity Ajan Prasit had stood for, how that and my love for Wichai had occupied my life so fully. And how it all seemed so frail a fabric to weave my life upon now. Here was a madman and his single- and simple-minded sidekick, with an obsession I couldn't dent with any logic. Or compassion. We were Ben's puppets for the moment, as surely as he felt he was pulled on strings held by those above him. I didn't like the feeling at all.

The acrid smoke of early-morning fires drifted just over the placid waters of the Chee River as we stepped and slid down its slimy bank. A boat was tied up there, a simple affair with a small motor, which Ben started as Tawit sat glaring at us from the bow.

Wichai reached for my hand and weaved my fingers into his as Ben pushed off and headed us upriver.

"My family will worry, Ajan Peter," he said above the sound of the motor. "We will be missed at the festival."

I squeezed his hand in mine. "I know, Wichai. This will be over soon."

At the bridge we left the boat and waited for a bus. When one came clamoring up, we hailed it and squeezed inside. It is somewhat euphemistic to call such a vehicle a bus, I thought. An old truck bed with a teak frame built around it, holding hard, wooden benches, it was filled with villagers on the way to market with their animals and produce. I was forced between Ben and Tawit. Wichai was shoved up against a woman nursing her infant son. The clucking of chickens rose above the engine as they rode in their straw cages on the roof. A number of passengers spit betel to the floor as they eyed us in the darkness of the cramped interior.

Ben seemed to sleep as we bounced along, but Tawit was on guard, his eyes beady-bright and intense. Wichai leaned back and closed his eyes, too. I felt tense, unable to let go and surrender control over the situation. How could I get Wichai away from this maniac?

We got into Banpai, with all the noise and furor common with arrival at market. Ben jerked awake, his eyes searching for a scene he recognized. They found me, then looked to Tawit, and I could see purpose return to them, and terror.

"We go north to Nong Khai from here, Pete," he said flatly as we got out. "Then a boat across the Mekong to Laos and I figure I'm gone, gone from the war, gone from Fisher, fucking gone from the world."

"We take the train from here?" I asked. This was the town where people from Roi-Et always used to transfer to rail for journeys north or south.

"Naw," said the man. "Feel like a sitting duck in that thing. Besides, they register names of passengers. Don't want to give Fisher a scent of our trail."

He motioned for Wichai and me to walk ahead to the line of buses parked beside the train station. Wichai, still woozy from sleep, stumbled against me. Tawit moved forward, the point of his knife sinking into the boy's lower back.

Wichai gasped and winced with the stabbing pain. I spun on the Thai, my fist raised and clenched.

Ben grabbed my shoulders and spun me around, his fingers digging into my skin. Tawit withdrew his knife and we stepped forward again.

"Don't try anything, Pete old boy," Ben said grimly. "Tawit here thinks he's some sort of commando hero like he's seen in the kung fu Chinese movies. He'll slice you or your little friend to shreds if you try anything."

We sat in the growing heat, at the base of a crumbling wall surrounding the bus corral, waiting for the bus to Nong Khai. It's what people did a lot of in Thailand — wait. Patience was more a necessity than a virtue. Wichai and I were again separated by Tawit, who remained alert. I longed to talk with him, to feel him next to me. I felt terribly weak, but still struggled with the reality of being a hostage. There would be an opportunity to escape, I thought.

There was an excited yell, followed by a heavy splash of water over our heads. Ben jumped to his feet. Tawit yanked his knife out. I gasped aloud as the cool water cascaded over us.

It was a group of young boys behind us, giggling and jumping, their now empty buckets swinging in their hands. They giggled again, then ran off to refill their pails with more water at the pump.

"What the hell?" barked Ferrall. His jaw was set, waterdrops flung from his stubbled chin.

I braced myself. The man was crazy enough to try anything, especially with a prank like that played on him.

I looked to Tawit. I expected him to have his knife out, ready for action. Oddly, his expression was softened beneath his plastered-down hair, and his knife was once again in his belt.

"What is it?" I asked Wichai frantically.

"Songkran, Ajan Peter," he answered. "The water festival I told you about. It is a time when the people pour water on each other in thanksgiving for the return of the rains to the land. I told you it is much fun." His expression soured. "But now it is not so much fun."

The boys returned, pails brimming with water. All around us, I saw that people were getting their share of splashing, too. When the boys swung the buckets up, long silvery streams of water again flooded over us.

Ben stood there shaking with anger. I hurriedly explained the custom, and he fought to control himself. But I watched from the corner of my eye to see if the boys would return a third time. I checked Tawit's posture. Wichai was relaxed, reliving, perhaps, the memory of happier Songkran Festivals as the water soaked him.

As the boys ran up a third time, Ben did what I thought he might. He turned on them, shouting almost hysterically. Tawit was distracted by the man's public display of anger —something Thais did only at the risk of disgrace—and I saw my chance.

I dived past the bandit and grabbed Wichai's hand. Springing away, I dragged the boy until he gained his footing and was running alongside me toward the market. Ben's rage was turned from the boys onto me as we weaved through baskets and under tarps, trying to lose ourselves in the morning crowd.

Along rows of straw baskets we sped, tipping some over and getting more water sprayed on us as we ran and slid through the milling shoppers. Fishy smells assaulted us, then the fruit stands, all whizzing by in a kaleidoscope of color as Wichai and I sprinted through the market.

"You bastard!" Ben yelled behind us. "You frigging bastard. Don't desert me, you asshole. I ain't going to let you leave me here!"

It was as much a plea for help as a command for us to stop. But I didn't let his tone slow us down. Especially with his buddy and his knife.

"This way," said Wichai, and tugged me to the right.

We ran down a narrow path, a low wall on one side and the side of a shop on the other. I could hear footsteps right behind us.

"Here, in here!" gasped the boy. We rounded a corner and skidded through the gates of the wall. We were in a temple compound, the building itself rising up before us with its dazzling reds and greens. Wichai had led us to the one place his training told him there would be sanctuary, where evil and danger dare not follow.

I had hardly breath nor time to tell him different when Tawit fell on my back, knocking me to the ground. Ben was right behind. He grabbed Wichai and locked his arms painfully behind his back.

Struggle was futile, but I tried to punch a vulnerable spot as he landed on me. I nicked his chin and threw him off balance. Briefly. He was very strong, his flesh tightly bound into muscle, and he attacked me like a cat. I went limp under the man and felt tears of frustration burning down my cheeks into the dust.

When I looked up I saw that Ben had bound Wichai's arms behind him with a chord of jute. He pushed the boy to the ground and came up to me. His boot went into my nose.

Sharp, penetrating pain rang through my skull. He kicked again, then again. He stopped and dropped to his knees beside me.

"Oh, shit, Pete, I'm sorry," he said with a breaking voice. "I don't want to hurt anyone ever again. Shit, if you'd only do as I told you, you fucking asshole. I'm sorry. . . ." His voice trailed off into a wheezing gurgle as he weaved back and forth on his knees.

I felt blood burning down my nostrils and over my split lip. The man was so unstable, I didn't know what to expect. The fight had certainly gone out of me for the time being, so I just lay limp, trying to let it go, just let it go.

Finally, Ben settled down. He reached for a pack at his belt and snapped it open. "Hold him tight," he told Tawit as he withdrew a hypodermic and a small brown vial. He rammed the needle into the cork of the vial and pulled the plunger back.

"Got some special medicine for ya, Pete," he said in a monotone. "Got it from the village doc back at Bantawat. It's something keeps me company all the time now, Pete old boy, and I figure it's time you enjoy some of it yourself."

While Tawit held me down, he pulled up my sleeve, thumbed up my bicep, and stabbed the needle in deep.

A surge of warmth enveloped me. A dreamy expansion of vision bubbled up all around, filled with lush color and life. I tasted honey and smoke on my tongue. The narcotic drowned what was left of my anger, and sucked the fight from my guts. I was left feeling numb and passive.

133

"Come on," said Ben as he and his buddy pulled me to my feet. "We got a bus to catch."

All I remember from the bus ride north is a blur of the rice fields as we sped past, and of an occasional shower of warm, soothing water as we came to a group beside the road celebrating the Songkran tradition. That, and, more than anything, I remember Wichai. He seemed to be raised out of the daze that shaded everything else, as though he were a living bas-relief. He was real, and his eyes spoke his fear — and his hope — as they looked into mine.

22

Ben punched the drug into me once more before we pulled into Nong Khai. What I remember of the rest of that day is pretty hazy, but I do recall coming out of my daze in a hotel room with Wichai beside me on the floor and the two men drinking whiskey at a crude table. Our backs were against the wall. From Wichai's expression, I couldn't tell whether he'd been drugged too, or had just withdrawn into himself.

"Are you all right?" I asked the boy quietly.

Wichai glanced at the men, then to me. "Yes, Ajan Peter. I was worried about you. I didn't know if you would wake up."

"Where are we?"

"Nong Khai, in a hotel by the river," he whispered. "We must wait until morning to get a boat across the Mekong. No boats travel the river at night; it is too dangerous with the war so close."

Squinting seemed to help bring things more into focus. And the voices in the room began to ring less hollowly as the drug wore off.

Wichai handed me a glass of tea. "Are you well, Ajan Peter?" he asked.

"I'm all right. Just tired and confused," I said, then gulped down the tea. I reached to my neck for the Buddha image given to me by the priest the night Wichai and I made love in the waters of the gulf. It felt cool and reassuring, and the memories living in it gave me hope somehow. We didn't have much else to grab hold of.

The boy and I listened to the slurring words of the two men for a while. I didn't even try to make sense out of them, just felt the tension crackling in their voices.

"I think we will be safe," said Wichai finally, "if we do what they say."

I nodded. He was trying to tell me to take it easy, to be Thai, more passive in the face of superior strength. He used the word *maipenrai*, which is the equivalent of 'keep cool,' among other things.

I understood. "I won't try to escape again, Wichai," I said. "I don't want to get us killed trying."

He merely nodded. His eyelids were heavy with sleep. "Ajan Peter," he said with slow determination, "I think when we get back to Roi-Et I will become a monk for a while."

The evening slipped into night. Wichai was asleep where he sat at my side. His head fell forward, his legs spread out with his feet splayed, ankles against the wood. Tawit, with a smaller body and less tolerance than Ferrall, fell forward with drink and slept with his head in his arms. Ben sat hunched over and hummed to himself under the one light in the room, draining and refilling his glass of whiskey from time to time. Then he turned to me, as though just then aware that I was awake and watching him.

"Well, a fine state of affairs we've come to, eh, Pete old boy?" he said drunkenly. "Stuck here in this hole, deep in Asia, surrounded by enemies and — and looking at what?"

"The future?"

"Bah! Fuck the future!" He bolted the rest of his drink. "Never had no future anyways. And what future does America have here anyway? Saw a missionary once. He'd lived in Asia for somethin' like fourteen years. Think that'd give a man time to become a part of the place, eh? You know what that bastard did?"

I shook my head.

"Lived in his bungalow all week, never went out. Sent his boy out for stuff all the time and never showed his bright, blue nose. Then on Sundays the bastard would get into his Land Rover and drive around the province, throwing tracts out the window! Into the wind! That's our holy mission, Pete! To pollute the place!"

"But he was a missionary," I said. "He was trying to change them. I think we could live here if we just wanted to live together and learn from each other."

Ben fixed me with a glassy stare. "Idealistic bullshit!" he spat. He gulped again. "Kipling was right, Pete — East and West and all that. My daddy was right, too. Can't win a war in Asia, he used to say. It wouldn't be clean like it was in Europe, he said." He reached for Tawit's half-full glass and held it out to me. "You want some poison?"

I took it as an invitation to join him. Why not play his game? My legs were a bit rubbery, but I managed to stand and walk over to the table. My muscles were not capable of any more than that. I pulled out a chair and sat, and sipped the bitter whiskey. "Thanks, Ben," I said.

He leaned over the table and put a sweaty hand heavily on my arm. "I don't want to kill you, Pete, and not your friend neither. But I got to if it means business. My ass, Pete. That's what I got to save. If there's trouble, if those bastards try anything, Fisher or any of 'em, I'll. . . ."

"There won't be any trouble," I attempted. But I could see my words did nothing to temper his paranoia. I changed the subject. "What did you do before the war, Ben?"

He lifted his head to the light and narrowed his eyes, as if it demanded physical effort to remember a life prior to Nam. "Jesus, Pete, that was a long time ago. Just before I enlisted, I was working at a lumberyard. Good job, too, and had me a nice Chevy, and gettin' serious with a girl named Vicki. My folks were crazy about her. She used to tease my daddy, when we'd barbecue out back, and he'd tease my Vicki right back. They were a pair, my girl and my daddy. I loved that woman.

"I didn't think I was good enough for her, really. She'd moved from Memphis with her folks when her daddy's real estate office changed his territory, a big-city girl. The war came along and my daddy started to hint about how he'd fought in the war. And Vicki would look at me like I wasn't a man unless I served my country, too.

"Ma didn't want me to sign up, but daddy said it was up to me, that I was a man now. Vicki said she'd get a job with my daddy till I got back, that she'd write me every week and wait for me."

I watched as a mosquito lit on Ben's cheek, poised, then punctured the skin. He didn't wince as its belly swelled with blood.

"I was proud. They sent me to classes, trained me for secret missions. There was a shortage of men then, before Johnson started cutting 'em loose. I was elite. And I fought, too! I bet I got more killing in a month than my daddy did in the whole war.

"Vicki stopped writing," he wheezed.

A motorcycle passed under our window, its raw motor spitting sound.

"Fuck her."

He went on talking. The reminiscences became largely non sequiturs, brief vignettes into his life that I soon lost track of. My eyes felt heavy, and the whiskey was anesthetic, especially on top of the aftereffects of the drug. I leaned forward with my chin on my arms for a while. I soon fell asleep with his words droning through my head.

23

What woke me was a sharp prick of pain in my arm. It was Ben with another hypodermic. I merely groaned. I just wanted it to be over now. I didn't want to fight any more. Never did my life with Wichai and Ajan Prasit at Roi-Et seem more idyllic and I wondered, as the drug seeped through my consciousness, why I had never been more grateful for those moments.

We managed to walk to the river, just a couple blocks away. Ben and Tawit more or less supported me, while the Thai kept a firm hold on Wichai. If anyone saw us, it would appear that a man and his son were kindly helping two farang, one of them drunk, find their way to the boats that ferried the Mekong.

There was a quivering tenseness in the hands guiding me along, and I could see Ben swing his eyes left and right, on the lookout for any sign of trouble.

"Passports, please," said the immigration officer at the small wooden office on the wharf. Ben fished mine out of my pocket and they were all laid open for inspection, along with Wichai's papers.

It was hot and sticky as we watched the man peruse them with deliberate authority. No shower the night before, none this morning—that and the effects of the drug had my skin itchy and my head heavy.

The official didn't look up as he spoke. "Your purpose for going to Vientiane?"

"A visit," said Ben. "We need to restock our supply of liquor." He gave a wink which the man didn't bother to look up to see.

The officer nodded, slowly turning a page. Vientiane was a duty-free port. The reason would no doubt seem reasonable.

"How long will you stay in Laos?"

"A couple days," Ben lied.

I looked sideways at Wichai. He had rested his free hand on the counter. As drugged as I was, it seemed I saw him move his fingers to signal the man behind the counter. Perhaps it was something typically Thai, perhaps nothing. Regardless, the official closed each passport, then stood. "I must make a phone call first," he said. "To check with security. The market in Vientiane was bombed two days ago."

We waited nervously. The rich odor of river-rotting greens hung in the air, almost making me sick. My head was swimming.

When the officer returned, he immediately stamped our papers and handed them back. "Sorry for the delay, sirs," he said with a perfunctory smile.

We boarded the boat and sputtered into the current of the Mekong. My head was ringing and darkness swarmed around the corners of my vision.

In contrast, Ben and Tawit were excited at leaving the shores of Thailand. Their goal was in sight, tantalizingly close. "There it is, Tawit," said Ferrall, his wild eyes on the banks of Laos, "our ticket to a good life."

The Thai struck an heroic stance at the bow and grinned. He pulled out his knife. "A great warrior, Ben, yes?" be boasted.

A bullet rang against the blade and almost flung it from his grip. We all turned to the direction it came from and saw a military police boat churning up water toward us. I squinted. On deck, with a rifle pointed at us, swam the figure of Mark Fisher. No mistaking his blond hair. It flew like a golden flag as he peered down the scope of his rifle right at us.

"Shit!" shouted Ben. He grabbed for Wichai, who was closer, and held the boy close against him as he dug in his

140

belt for his gun. Tawit quickly pulled me between his heaving chest and the approaching boat. He held me firmly, and I more than covered him. There was no fight in me now. It was time for the hostages to play their role, I dimly thought.

The police boat cut across our bow. Its wake made us all fight for footing. The sun seemed to wash the scene almost to white, and I struggled to remain conscious.

"Give it up, Ferrall!" cried Fisher. "This is the end of the line. Let Peter and the boy go and we'll talk things over."

"No way!" yelled Ben. " 'Talk things over!' Fuck you! You mean take me in for a stretch in the pen. Or the grave, you bastard! Move that boat, or the blood of these two is on your hands!"

I could feel the force of each word drum through me in the thick air. I felt I was suffocating.

"It's over, Ferrall," came Fisher's sure voice across the churned-up water. "You've killed enough. And there's no way we're going to let you run around with what you know."

"Move it, bastard!" Ben answered. He jabbed the barrel of his gun up under Wichai's chin.

"No!" I heard myself scream. "Don't do it!"

I torqued around with what strength I had left, trying to shake Tawit off me. The boat tipped as he grabbed me back. His foot caught on the ribbing of the boat and he stumbled sideways. There was a flash from Fisher's gun and the heavy splat of lead slamming into Tawit's chest. He was knocked back by the impact, then bounced forward off the cabin onto me. We fell flat, the Thai on top of me.

"You bastard," I heard Ben shout. "You fuckin' bastard! I'm going to kill you!"

Tawit was not heavy, but I was so weakened by the drugs that his body was enough to hold me down. All I could do was twist and raise my head to see Ben turn his gun onto the police boat. Wichai seemed like a beautiful doll in his grip, his arms pulled up tight behind him.

A shot rang out. Then another. But the boat was rocking, and his gun was not as powerful nor as accurate as the CID man's rifle.

141

"I'll kill you!" he repeated, and put the hot metal again to Wichai's throat.

"Just like you killed those villagers, that little baby?" answered the voice of Mark Fisher from a long way away. "That baby with your face on it? Your blood? Maybe you wound up killing yourself, Ferrall? What would your daddy think of that, Ferrall?"

Ben's face underwent a horrible transformation. First shock, then imploding fear. His jaws trembled as his face screwed into a lined grimace. It was as though every nerve of his body was trying to fight off the searing sting of that memory. He was losing control. Tremors shook him. It seemed hours passed as I looked up at him, holding Wichai tight, battling for the ability to continue, to fight back further.

"Nooooooo!" he wailed. His finger closed on the trigger. With a monumental effort, I reached and grabbed at his leg. His gun went off. The explosion seemed to burst in my brain. I looked up. Blood already oozed from Wichai's shoulder. His eyes were wide with fear. Then they seemed to dim.

Ben flung the boy from him, hard enough to send him over the side, into the river.

There was an immediate blast from Mark's rifle. Ben was blown back, it seemed, in an action that was like multiple frames of a movie, each motion separate and blending inevitably into the next. A gaping hole, full of blood and shredded intestines, blossomed open from his belly. His eyes remained fixed and open as his spasming fingers dropped the gun to the bottom of the boat.

Wichai! he was hurt, and in the water, perhaps already dead or drowning. I clawed at the side of the boat, squirming from under Tawit's lifeless body, trying to grasp my way over the edge. I had to save the boy I loved, who had taught me so much, who had saved me from despair.

No use! A throbbing darkness pushed me back and down. It was like fighting a gravity ten times normal. Red shadows washed over me. I hit my head on the bottom of the bow and felt nothing.

There was a cool, dry hand stoking my cheek. As I came to, I felt the fingers run lightly down my chest and touch the image of Buddha lying chained around my neck. My own groan sounded distant as I pried my eyes open. Wichai was there, sitting beside the bed, touching me.

"Wichai," I managed to say, "you're alive!"

"Hush, Ajan Peter," came the boy's resonant voice in an echo.

He *was* alive! I cried with relief and happiness as he caressed me. I felt thick-headed and foolish, joyous and free all at the same time.

"Where are we?" I managed to ask.

"Nong Khai Hospital, Ajan Peter. I was hurt only a little," he said, turning his shoulder to show me a clean dressing. His arm was in a sling. "You have been resting for two days."

Two days? And still the drug pulled on me. But after I sipped tea from the glass Wichai held to my lips, I felt better, stronger.

"I thought you were killed," I sighed. "Or drowned in the river."

"I was hurt. And I was drowning. But Mr. Fisher jumped into the water and pulled me onto his boat. He put a bandage around here," he motioned to his arm, "and brought us to the hospital."

"Mark Fisher saved you?" I asked, incredulous.

"Yes, Ajan Peter. He put his mouth over mine and breathed air into me." The boy pulled a card from his shirt pocket. "He told me to give this to you, to see him in Bangkok next time you visit." He handed it to me and I put it on the tray beside my bed.

I felt relief replacing my fatigue. It was over. We were silent. My hand found his and I held it over my chest. There was time to order my thoughts some. Ben Ferrall was dead. Mark Fisher had killed him. And had saved Wichai from drowning.

Fisher the good guy? In a way, but nothing was so clear as it once was. It was like yin and yang, each spinning out their fate, each a part of the other to forever confound the best-intentioned absolutist. Ben Ferrall was 'good;' but had done bad things for the wrong reasons. And what was good and bad, right and wrong?

And me? I needed to examine my own motives more closely before I was sure of anything. There was too much madness in me now.

24

Two months passed after our return to Roi-Et before Thot Katin, Buddhist Lent. This marked a time for reevaluation in the lives of many Thais, of leaving old ways and beginning new. So it was for me and especially for Wichai.

Leading up to Thot Katin, life became pleasantly routine. Pra Anan had returned to his post at Songkhla. The new Headmaster was comfortably in charge of the college. Wichai and I returned to our duties as student and teacher with an ease which surprised me. We had both grown up some, but there were thankfully no traumatic effects left from our little adventure.

I often thought about Ben Ferrall's words, when he accused me of idealistic bullshit. He was speaking from a crazed cynicism I hoped never to approach; but he was pretty close to the mark on that one in some ways, I had to admit. My initial despair had been as a yin that flipped to the yang of the newly converted, where I saw only the good and virtuous in Thailand and its people. Now, I hoped, I was gaining a more balanced outlook.

Wichai and I had grown together almost as family. Our love, if anything, was more substantial than ever. We were bonded by so many people and events now, and had endured some adversity with no regrets. Wichai's physical attractions were only heightened by his calm and courageous spirit. Our passion was but one facet of our love, an essential one, for we were two males in the fire of youth; but I was content to merely know he loved me, and that he trusted me to love him.

This was important, for the time approached for me to return to America. May and June passed, with the monsoons sending more billowing clouds over the flat landscape, to tease awake the parched earth with gushing rains. I would leave in July.

"Ajan Peter, you remember what I said in Nongkai about becoming a monk?" Wichai asked as we sipped orange drinks after classes.

"Yes," I answered. "Do you still intend to do it?"

"I feel I must. I want to earn merit for me and my family, and I want to learn how to be a better Buddhist," he said seriously. "When life changes very fast, when there is violence to the natural order of growth, it is best to enter the monastery and restore that order."

Wichai, still with the body of a boy, was indeed becoming a man.

"When will you do it?" I asked.

"Buddhist Lent will be next month. I will ordinate then. I want you to be there with my family when I enter the monastery."

"I will, Wichai. Then I will return to my home." As we sat there, sipping the cool drinks and watching the campus activity diminish with evening falling around us, I thought about what the boy had just said. "What is merit, Wichai? How do you earn it?"

"You have heard the saying 'Do good, receive good,' Ajan Peter. It is the law of cause and effect, like they teach us in physics: we do good deeds and we receive rewards. If we do evil, bad things will happen to our spirits. Karma is simply that — cause and effect."

How simple. "You are punished for doing bad deeds, then?"

Wichai smiled winningly. "We are punished *by* our sins, I think, not *for* them. A man cannot be serene while his spirit is troubled with evil. Therefore he suffers until he earns merit to lift him above the misery he has caused himself."

146

"Cause and effect," I mused. "Like physics."

"The natural world obeys the same laws, we are taught, whether it is in matter or in mind," the boy said, struggling to find the proper fashion of phrasing it. He tried another illustration, "When I become a monk and you return to your home, we will smooth out the rough edges of the universe made when Ajan Prasit died, and when we experienced violence in Nong Khai. The full cycle will be complete."

I nodded, comprehending the simplicity of it all. I pointed to my head. "The universe?"

Wichai eagerly nodded.

"You are a good teacher, Wichai."

Now he smiled with pride. Then the grin turned impish. "Tonight I will also teach you something new," he said.

Before I could reply, the boy reached into his pocket and pulled out a tube. I raised my eyebrows.

"Cocoa-palm cream, Ajan Peter," he said almost in a whisper. "It is a special love oil I got from my friend in the market!"

There is no specific date for Lent; it is determined by astrological means, and this year fell in mid-July. For three months, all over Thailand, young men would enter the monastery for training and meditation. As important as learning priestly duties, this is seen as a rite of passage proclaiming a boy's journey into manhood; family and community pride is demonstrated at the ordination, and Wichai's was an event which proved to me the extent they honored him.

More significant, Wichai's ordination was to be the first held at the newly completed temple Ajan Prasit had devoted himself to in the last days of his life. The village and college both were bustling with the activities which would blend the final dedication of the temple, Buddhist Lent, with Wichai's entrance into priestly service.

The night before his ordination, we lay on our backs in bed, the pure light of a full moon streaming in the windows and through cracks in the boarded walls. The mosquito netting around us performed a slow dance in the breeze.

"Listen," Wichai said. "Do you hear it?"

I listened, only hearing the descending croak of a gecko somewhere under the house. Then, there it was. Softly at first, just on the verge of hearing, so sweet I felt it must be my imagination. Then stronger, changing tones and rising high above us.

"Kite music!" the boy said, and rolled over to embrace me.

I held the boy tight, running my lips over his neck. My hand rose up along his lean back, feeling every muscle and bone respond to my touch. After caressing the nape of his neck, I rested my hand over his finely shaped head, feeling for the first time his newly shaven skull.

"A monk is like an old man," he laughed into my shoulder, "homeless and bald."

The smooth touch of his bare head was erotic. I kissed his face, and my lips slipped over his shaven eyebrows. His hair had been cut to the skin that day in preparation for his ordination, and would be like all monks every full moon after that.

Except for his sparse pubic patch, the boy was totally hairless. He told me of the reasons for the custom: to unite the brotherhood of monks in a similar appearance, and to reduce any vanity that comes with grooming. But to me his smooth body was more seductively tempting than ever. Perhaps my appetites were heightened by the knowledge that this night would be our last such embrace. Maybe the kite music was an aural aphrodisiac as well.

By the time we fell apart, damp with sweat and smelling of semen and Wichai's cocoa-palm oil, it was very late.

25

The day of the ceremonies was dazzling bright, and the spectrum of colors at the temple challenged nature's lush production. Wichai was bright and cheerful, glad the day he had so long prepared for had arrived.

In the monks' quarters of the temple, the boy and I were alone together for the last time.

"You must follow every step, Ajan Peter," he smiled. "If I forget because I am nervous, you must remember everything."

"I will," I promised.

He wore the initiate's costume of a simple garment, bleached white and unadorned, which would be exchanged at the ordination chapel for his monk's saffron robe. He had studied with the abbot and practiced with me the words he would speak, and felt confident in going through the process smoothly.

I stood back for a long look. I wanted to burn the presence of him deep into my memory. Then I took an object from my shirt pocket and held it out. "I have a gift for you."

He took the small, tissue-wrapped package and opened it. It was an image of the Buddha, similar to the one I wore around my neck.

"It is very beautiful, Ajan Peter. Thank you."

"The abbot gave it to me, Wichai," I said. "He told me he had taken one of Ajan Prasit's teeth from the funeral pyre and put it in the Buddha."

149

Wichai shook it gently at his ear to hear the relic rattle within it. "Thank you," he said with a deep wai I returned. There were tears in his eyes. He held his arms open and we held each other for a long time.

That was the closest we came to saying good-bye. I left him to prepare himself and went to the road leading to the market with colleagues who wanted to make this an occasion for my farewell feast as well. We ate and drank lavishly in the town's best restaurant—not the best looking, for it was shabbier than most. But it had the finest food, cooked over steaming woks by a Mama Seesin, with all her brood of children looking on.

My fellow teachers in the English Department lauded my work. I praised them for their example and help. Then the talk moved to stories of my time there, then, with the beer, became full of the exaggerations common to people who seldom reveal their true emotions in public.

One celebration ended as another began. We heard the drums beating in the street and went out. First came the parade of Thot Katin, a long line through the streets of Roi-Et, Laotians in their native costumes, proud Boy Scouts, and self-important provincial officials. Each carried the gifts they would present to the temple: new robes, soap, cigarettes, and offering bowls. And branches from the tamarind tree, each sprouting blossoms made from colorful baht notes.

There was music, the joyous folk rhythms of beating drums and pan pipes, along with the songs sung by strong, young voices. Graceful girls swayed through the growing heat of the day as they performed dances learned in childhood. Long silver fingernails enhanced the backward bend of their slender fingers. I traveled along the parade route with the college staff, with a loose line of happy students trailing along behind us. Never had I felt more as though I truly belonged here. And the irony was that I was about to leave. Perhaps it was just as well, that I depart at the point where the country and its people were no longer exotically Asian to me. Perhaps I would become complacent if I remained, and not apply what I'd learned to new challenges.

We arrived at the temple in time to see Wichai arrive from the monks' quarters riding a small, white horse. His eyes were down. He seemed oblivious to the clamor of the crowd all around him as the horse was led around the temple clockwise three times. His friends shouted encouragement and his family followed directly behind. I spotted his mother and father and walked up beside them. We made deep wais and smiled proudly at each other. It was impossible to talk above the noise of fireworks and yelling.

After Wichai's final circuit, his horse was brought to a halt before the ordination chapel. The boy dismounted and was led to his knees in front of the building by the lay priest of the village. he was a venerable old man, wise, it was said, in the ways of medicine and fortune telling.

As they knelt, the lay priest led my young lover through a series of questions, part of his initiation rite before leaving the outside world.

"I must disclaim any possessions," Wichai had told me. "And vow to remain within the temple during the season of Lent. We must always do good to receive good, Ajan Peter; but only as a monk can a man hope to attain nirvana, and that is what I must promise to strive toward."

There must have been more to it, for it went on for some minutes. When they stood, there was a buzz from the crowd. I squeezed into the packed little chapel just behind his family as Wichai was led to the raised platform before the altar. Other monks of the temple sat around the perimeter of the platform, but he stood before the abbot.

Wichai had told me about this, too: "I will take the vows of the brotherhood inside the chapel. I must promise to renounce all worldly pursuits and enter into the brotherhood of the temple with clear purpose. We will speak in Pali, the language of the Lord Buddha."

As Wichai and the abbot followed the ancient ritual, another monk assisted in exchanging the initiate's clothing into the robes of a priest. The boy look so beautiful, wonderfully adorned in the simple folds of his saffron cloth, elegantly humble, yet with poise which revealed his nimble energy of mind and body. That robe, an offering bowl, and a sieve were all the possessions he would be allowed during his stay in the monastery. He would require nothing else.

A feast followed Wichai's ordination. I joined with my colleagues in eating the tasty variety of spicy dishes, then finished up with a variety of fruits and coconut puddings. Above us, the monks dined deliberately on their noon meal, and I watched from a distance now as Wichai ate with quiet contemplation, keeping his large, dark eyes appropriately lowered.

The day was not complete until the temple had been dedicated, and the auspicious moment was deemed to fall at sundown. So after a late afternoon's rest, most who had been there throughout the day gathered again at the temple, this time with candles, incense, and flowers in their hands.

I don't remember much of the ceremony, I'm afraid. By the time the last speech was made, the temple blazed with candles. They were clustered on the walls surrounding it so it appeared like some gigantic celebration cake set in the midst of the tropical forest. Whiskey was offered along with the food, and I drank enough to be left with blurry memories of that night.

Except one. When the monks again chanted, candlelight glowing on their serene faces and the compound sweet with incense, I looked up at Wichai. I saw in him the young boy, so eager and shy, who first came to my home as a barefoot villager; I saw also the young man I lusted for, and finally touched. And I saw the more mature Wichai, facing danger and bigotry with a dignity beyond his years. And then the present, final image — the young disciple, calmly expressionless, wisely meditative.

Wichai raised his head slowly and his eyes found mine. His lips hinted at a smile — and he winked!

BOOKS FROM BANNED BOOKS

Kite Music,
Gary Shellhart $8.95
Mountain Climbing in Sheridan Square,
Stan Leventhal $8.95
Skiptrace,
Antoinette Azolakov $8.95
A Cry in the Desert,
Jed A. Bryan $9.95
Cass and the Stone Butch,
Antoinette Azolakov $8.95
Dreams of the Woman Who Loved Sex,
Tee Corinne $7.95
Tangled Sheets,
Gerard Curry $7.95
Death Strip,
Benita Kirkland $8.95
Days in the Sun,
Drew Kent $8.95
Fairy Tales Mother Never Told You,
Benjamin Eakin $5.95

These books are available from your favorite bookstore or directly from:

BANNED BOOKS
Number 231, P.O. Box 33280, Austin, Texas 78764

Add 15% of order total for postage and handling. Texas residents, please add 8% sales tax.